THE MOONLIT DANCE

ZOE ABRAMS

THE MOONLIT DANCE

ZOE ABRAMS

A word to the reader…

The Moonlit Dance is a work of fiction, however there are some real-world situations throughout the book that might be sensitive to some readers. This book contains themes of sex and imprisonment. The main characters experience a ton of growth through book one and book two. This book does have a happily ever after! This book is intended for audiences over the age of eighteen and features a why choose romance including MMF, MFM, and MF pairings. Please be kind to yourselves!

Much love,

Zoe

AVAN

My consciousness faded in and out. Flashes of gray eyes and pink lips, a wry smile, a soft chuckle. Large hands wrapped tightly in a sheet of dark hair. Cal and Briar tangled in each other's embrace. I wanted to hold onto that vision forever.

The steady drip, drip, drip of water drew my attention from where I'd been staring at the sky. The visions of Briar were interspersed with memories of this very cell. The bite of the manacles brought me back to the time I'd spent here before, when the council locked me away the first time. *Sedition.* I spat at the word. How could one be accused of trying to overthrow the crown when they were supposed to be king in the first place?

A soft snore drew my attention to where Cal's form hung limply, wrists chained to the wet walls, his chest rising and falling in a soft rhythm. The tempered magic within me swirled slowly and angrily at the sight, almost every drop sucked into the golden bangles around my wrists as I ached to reach towards my oldest companion. That small green swirl threading through me was what was going to save us. I huffed, tilting my head back to my perusal of the waning moon. It crept slowly through the sky, stars blinking in and out of existence around it. All this trouble, caused by one catastrophic prophecy made years ago.

I could still smell the rancid air in that traveling charade of a circus. Their carmisles weren't even wild, the small tusks notating that they were born in captivity. No wild beasts like their posters claimed, no true fortune weavers. That specific magical trait had been bred out centuries before even Morina was born.

That teller, though, he had the blood in him—however minuscule—and when his blue eyes went glassy and unfocused, I saw the future play out in them. Scene after scene, whizzing by in his mind's eye before landing on the one thing that destroyed my future.

"You will bring to light the destruction of us all. The catalyst for the annihilation of magic as we know it, grasped within your hands."

The words rang in my ears for weeks as I mulled them over. It was straightforward, but still – the annihilation of magic as we know it? I had to put a stop to whatever it was. So, into the library I dove, hunting down ancient tomes filled with long forgotten magic. It was a simple tracking spell, designed to cage whatever the magic sought. I thought it would have been a sort of relic, that finding and destroying it would erase the curse cast upon me—all with a simple incantation and an offering of blood.

Ian had other ideas.

"You're still the most powerful of us all, Av. So what if you aren't the king?"

"You have to put this ritual out of your mind. What if the council found

out? Do you think Cal would approve?"

"You're an idiot."

All attempts at talking me out of the ancient blood magic ritual went in one ear and out the other. Something could be said about my bullheadedness, but it wouldn't come from my lips. As he magicked away to the citadel to try and override me, the pompous fool, I swore before the ancient witches' cavern and gave my sacrifice.

I can still feel the magic ripping from me with each drop of blood on that old cavern floor, rushing out into the world to destroy anything that stood in the way of my reign. It had to have worked, I thought as I laid there on that uncomfortable stone floor, until the council descended inside that cavern and ripped away almost whatever was left of the evergreen magic within me. I was weak from the spell I'd just performed, all my strength barreling out into the world. If I could just make them see—the destruction was gone!—they would have sung my praises from the rooftops.

Maybe even crown me sooner.

But no. It hadn't worked, the spell leaving only death left in its wake. I could still see the two sets of unseeing eyes staring back at me in the Queen's atrium, two common witches at the end of the most dangerous spell I'd ever cast. They only had household magic, settled away in a secluded corner of the kingdom but dead, nonetheless. Nothing about them screamed "the annihilation of magic". Maybe I'd just invoked the spell wrong.

Regardless, I had to pay for my crimes. I was shuttled away to the deepest recesses of the citadel, Cal joining me shortly after a failed escape attempt. His judgment came in the form of banishment—his mind sent into the void and body left in a suspended state for decades. That is, until *she* came along and threw everything into chaos.

Briar.

I didn't even know Briar had completed her trials until the citadel captain arrived at our rooms—basically plush prison cells—and informed us we were officially under arrest for conspiracy against the crown. Again. Briar had escaped the dungeons somehow, and I was sure Ian had something to do with it. It was over quickly, our arrest. With the tempered magic of the bracelets, Cal and I had been helpless to the swarm of guards that trailed in after the captain.

That wasn't to say Cal went quietly. As they marched us through the atrium of the castle, he swung his arms back, catching the guard behind him in the nose. One determined look at me was all Cal gave before taking off towards the stairs to the city proper. A shot of gray magic trailed after him, striking him squarely in the back. The captain cast a glare at the guard behind him as he walked towards Cal's still body, looming over him before offering a hand to help him up.

"It'll be easier if you don't run," he'd said, a grimace stretching the scar across his face, almost begging him to behave. Cal pulled himself up, and I could tell the way his eyes darted to the captain's swords, he had another idea blooming in that scary brain of his.

I'd struggled against my captor, his hold on me tighter now that Cal had tried to run. "Cal. Don't," I shouted at him.

Our gaze met across the atrium, and I knew that look in his eyes. It didn't matter how much I struggled as Cal lunged for the dagger at the captain's waist, his head was knocked back again by that dark gray magic.

It was so similar to our last arrest, Cal vainly trying to be the hero, to his detriment. It was different now, though. Briar made it different. I didn't struggle as they hoisted up Cal's limp body, throwing out a spell to encase him in the same warded bubble I'd used before Briar brought him back from the void.

Through the mountains we went, days moving by as we traveled to Cesa. Each passing day, I made a list in my mind of people who might be willing to help their king.

So here I sit, in my cold, damp cell, plotting and planning. Each name was meticulously chosen for their loyalty to me, each plan weaved in and out until I was sure I had a solid one in place. The sun began peeking above the hole in the stone ceiling far above us, and determination bloomed in my chest. This would work. I would find Briar, save her from Ian's clutches, and she, Cal, and myself would live out our days far from Alehem.

I nudged Cal's knee until he woke, sapphire eyes blinking blearily in the early morning light. We had only been there overnight, one of the citadel guards using his magic to remove the stasis spell on Cal after they chained him.

"W'happened?" Cal mumbled. His eyes scanned the room, rounding as he peered up to where his wrists hung from the wall. "Avan, what the fuck happened?" Cal shook the manacles, the bracelets tightening as he tried and failed to use his magic.

"Calm down, Calvin. I have a plan," I murmured, tracking the sun as it rose in the sky. Our timing would have to be perfect. "The guard rounds should be the same. Sit still."

"I will burn this entire fucking citadel to the ground, Avan. Briar is gone, we've been arrested, and you're just sitting there, not telling me anything. Again," Cal huffed, rattling his chains against the stone. I rolled his eyes. Sometimes, Cal was so shortsighted, even more so with the enigmatic woman consuming both our thoughts.

"Patience is a virtue, my dear friend. You know as well as I that until these bracelets come off, we're sitting ducks." I eyed the golden circles around my wrist, gently twisting them to catch the sunlight now pouring into the cell.

"No, Avan, my patience has run out. I finally have something good in my life, and I'm not going to sit here while you brood and keep your secrets. Briar is out there somewhere with Ian and he's doing magic knows what to keep her hidden, and we're stuck here. So, open that big mouth of yours—I know you know how to use it—and fucking talk to me!" The chains shook from Cal lunging forward, a small jump in my chest the only thing alerting me to the danger mere feet away. "I'm so *fucking* tired of you not talking to me," he hissed through bared teeth.

I huffed out a soft breath, shaking my head as Cal continued to rage against the wall. My eyes skirted towards the sun again, only mere minutes until my tenuous plan clicked into place.

What surprised me the most, though, wasn't the sullen guard walking through the iron door. It was the golden captain a few steps behind him. A small change in plans.

"Gentleman, if you would be so kind as to not attack us, let's go have a chat in my office," he rumbled, nodding to the guard to unhook Cal from the wall. I rose silently, studying the scarred face in front of me. The captain flicked his gaze towards Cal before settling back on me and slightly nodding. Our trip upstairs was quick, the mid-morning sun illuminating the marble citadel. Scholars ran with stacks of papers floating in the air behind them as they shuffled from one end of the library to another.

Memories bubbled to the surface, ones of an enthusiastic, young would-be king floundering through these very halls. My time here was lonely, everyone too afraid to incur the wrath of the council if they misspoke, leaving me to myself more often than not. I built walls around my heart, hardening myself to the aching chasm of loneliness I felt. I threw myself into my studies, learning all I could about different magic and spells, wards and potions, anything I could get my hands on.

Then, one stormy night, a young knight found my snoozing form draped across a table in the furthest recesses of the library, candle long burnt out from my late-night studying. He gathered my notes and books, stacking them neatly for me to find later, and scooped me into his arms to deposit gently back in my room. The only hazy memory I had of the serendipitous meeting was a moonlit backdrop against a shock of bright red hair.

I didn't see him again for weeks, only brief glances of armor and red hair, freckles and a linen shirt around a corner. I tried asking my professors about him, but no one knew who the enigmatic knight was. It infuriated me—his wraith-like presence, the never-ending thoughts about what he looked like, his dreams, what he liked and disliked.

Until there he was, standing in the marble atrium with sunlight filtering through his fiery hair. He was speaking with a library assistant, folding a piece of paper between his slender fingers. I watched for a few moments behind a towering column before I spun to press my back into the marble, working up the nerve to mesh what I'd imagined in my head with the physical form.

"Excuse me."

I squeaked—embarrassingly loud, mind you—and turned towards

the voice. There he stood, all shining armor and cheeky grin.

"You're the scholar from the library, right? I've been meaning to find you. You left your notes and books, so I wanted to get them back to you." His smile widened as he looked me up and down, a heated expression blooming in his eyes.

After a very hot make-out session in the library, we met at least once a week for the next few months. I'd been all fumbling hands and knocking kisses, while his patience with me was saint-like. I'd never felt anything for anyone the way I burned for Cal.

I peered behind my shoulder at the person in question, the heated gaze in his eyes long gone and replaced with fury, often directed at me. I sighed, picking up my pace and leaving the memories behind.

The captain's office was cluttered, but clean. Neat stacks of paper adorned his desk in meticulous files, shelves of books lined the wall behind him, and a roaring fireplace shook the chill from the morning air. He sat behind his desk, scarred face turned into a scowl as he gestured for Cal and me to sit in the plush chairs in front of him. He nodded towards the other guard to stay in the hall, the soft snick of the door closing behind him.

He shuffled a few papers out of the way before placing a pair of small reading glasses on his nose, focusing his gaze on the correct form in front of him. "So, you two are back with more conspiracy charges, hmm?"

"Why aren't we being debriefed by the council, Captain? This seems a little above your pay grade," I drawled, leaning back into the comfy velvet. I could feel Cal's anger rolling off his body, but if my plan was going to work, I had to play the part.

"Evin, please. I think we're past formalities at this point," Evin sighed, leaning back into his chair. He chewed over his words for a moment before shuffling the papers on his desk, pulling out a crude drawing of Briar. "I saw the mistreatment of your friend, the way the council vilified her. I tried to help, in my own way, but she is quite stubborn." He chuckled softly, staring at the paper with a sort of awe I only saw reflected at myself in the mirror. "Ian took her before I could do anything, and it threw the council into a frenzy. With her powers just blooming, they're worried she's planning an attack."

"She doesn't even have full control of her powers!" Cal seethed. "What trouble could a fledgling witch be to the most powerful witches in the country?"

Evin and I glanced at each other, understanding passing between us. There were secrets I kept from Cal, and it seemed Evin at least had an inkling to what those were.

"As her powers grow with her coven, the council will become more and more wary of her. They want to cut the problem out at the root, before it becomes even bigger," Evin said.

"Her coven?" I asked.

"Are you not a part of her coven? I can sense her magic on you, even with the manacles." He glanced down at the offending golden circles. Interesting.

I had known the bond existed, obviously, but the fact that Briar had chosen us to be in her coven was news to me. What else could it be? It seems so simple, laid bare in front of me. She was mine. Ours. Forever.

"The little witchling deserves to be left in peace," Evin continued.

"Wherever she chooses to go, I'm going to ensure it." His eyes darkened, a soft twitch moving in his cheek. Did the captain…*like* Briar? This was going to be interesting.

"So, what? You want us to conspire *more* against the monarchy? Isn't that what we were thrown in those cells for? How do we know we can trust you?" I leaned forward, resting my elbows against my knees and threading my fingers together.

Cal sneered at me. "And yet, you expected Briar to trust you with little more than a word and a pretty smile. Tell me more," he said, turning towards the captain. Pretty, vicious man.

I wanted nothing to do with the monarchy, my mind and body tired after running for so long. The crown and council allowed me to live freely, muted as my powers are, but our tenuous peace was destroyed when they took Briar. Anger flared in my chest, dark emerald-green magic aching to pool in my palms. I held tight control over my powers, but when it came to Briar, I was a raging beast. This soft woman impacted me more than I ever thought possible. It didn't help that my relationship with Cal was strained due to my inaction.

I looked over to Cal, his gaze piercing mine, pleading with me to save the woman we…

"Briar needs protection, more protection than the dark witch can afford to spend on her. Ian is powerful, but she needs more than power to be safe." Evin's words echoed with double meaning, and I wondered again if the captain had more feelings towards Briar than he was letting on. "You know what atrocities the council has committed, and she's slighted them twice now: once with her successful completion of the trials, the other with her disappearance. I can't sit back and let them destroy her to save face."

"What you're suggesting is treason, dear captain," I drawled.

Evin scoffed and rolled his eyes. "You're going to sit here and tell me you haven't been plotting and planning an escape this whole time?"

I fought the uncomfortable bubble that rose in my chest at the—very true—accusation, but my lips stayed shut as I shot a glare his way.

"I'm offering you a way out of here—without bloodshed, mind you—and a way back to Briar," Evin explained.

"And what do you want from us?" Cal asked, his curious gaze darting between Evin and I.

"I want you to protect her with your lives. That's it." Evin shrugged.

There was always a catch, but I couldn't sense if Evin wanted anything else. I was usually a good reader of people, but his stoic mask was firmly in place. I couldn't help but be wary of the citadel captain suddenly taking an interest in my sweet witch.

"You don't believe me."

"I find it hard to believe you would give up everything for a witch you just met," I threw at him. I would break through that shell of his, damn it.

"Wouldn't you? Haven't you? You want to let her hide her powers away like Ian? Or do you want her to be safe, no matter where she goes? Briar is a rare witch, and she deserves to be free," Evin said.

Cal looked at me, nodding. He was already sold; anything that got him to Briar, come hell or highwater, he would be at her side. Wouldn't I do the same? A thin tendril of suppressed magic snaked through the dim bond we shared, and the empty hole in my heart ached to be filled.

"I'm listening."

BRIAR

It was nothing and everything, all at once. Moving between time and space never got any easier, the magic squeezing my lungs like a vice. My body was pulled after Ian's swirling magic, Jonas' hand grasping mine tightly until the bones ground together. Darkness swirled and pressed into my body until I could scarcely breathe, flashes of red hair and golden eyes swarming my vision before a scream ripped from my throat, the magic suddenly releasing me to the ground.

My gasps were harsh as I fought against the rising nausea, my grasping hands digging into the soft dirt underneath. As my breaths evened out, I rose onto my knees, thankful for solid ground. Jonas hadn't fared much better; his retching sounds to my side had the nausea rolling back in waves, threatening to pull me under.

"You'd never think you two were some of the most powerful witches of your generation," a snide voice said loudly. *Ian.* I glowered at him, wondering how hard I'd have to kick him to wipe that smirk off his face. My anger must amuse him, because his lips twitched at the look I shot him. Stupid witch and his stupid face.

"What the hell was that?" Jonas finally gained his voice back as I looked towards him, his tanned skin ghostly pale. He trembled as he reached towards my hand, grasping it tightly again. I grimaced, still sore from where he'd almost torn it off during the trip, but I swallowed my yelp at the look on his face.

I'd seen that look before, reflected at me in the mirror in a house far away, potions and concoctions lining the shelves behind me. That horrified, terror-stricken face was one I'd made as I learned more and more about the magic bubbling inside me, of the men surrounding me and the secrets they kept. I promised that girl I would find out the roots of my magic, even if it meant casting aside these blossoming feelings.

My mind thought back to — gods, had it just been a few minutes ago? — Cal and Avan's hands roaming over my body, whole and unblemished, far away from the council's reach. I could still taste them on my lips, and as I reached a shaky hand towards my face, Ian's sharp eyes flicked to the movement.

We met each other in that moment, his lips twisting and nose flaring, probably guessing what I was thinking about by the flare of his bond in my chest. I pulled my eyebrows together, daring him to speak. The smug smile shot my way told me he knew exactly where my mind had gone, and a burst of heat shot through me from where he stood.

"Briar?" Ian tilted his head towards Jonas, who was still desperately clasping my hand in his, shivers wracking his body until he was a trembling mess. I pulled his face to look at me and gasped. His pupils were blown, flicking back and forth, unseeing. Jonas' face was utterly white, drained of all color as his body trembled into full-blown convulsions.

"Jonas, you're going into shock. You need to breathe," I murmured to him, gently squeezing his cheeks in my hands. What I wouldn't do for a bit of Avan's magic right now…

I closed my eyes, reaching deep into my magic, and diving into some of that simmering lust still present. I gasped, tears springing into my eyes as I saw their magic swirling and twisting with mine, Cal's fire burning brightly. Avan's gentle earthy green swirled around Cal's in a caress, both twined in my dark smoky magic. I plucked and pulled the ties apart, coaxing Avan's magic to join mine fully. It was easy, way easier than stealing from Ian the few times I had, and his magic melded with mine until I could taste the explosion of spring on my tongue.

Emerald green filtered through my closed eyelids as I focused the magic through my hands to calm Jonas' panic. I opened my eyes, wonder filling me with the newest facet of powers I'd managed to unlock.

Jonas' breaths evened out, his pupils returning to a normal size before focusing on me. The light flicked and fizzled out as the last thread of Avan's power sputtered from existence.

"What…what did you just do to me?" he whispered, eyes darting around to…wherever we were.

"It's some of Avan's magic. I used it to calm you down, or else you were going to pass out. Do you feel better?" I asked.

Jonas nodded, his eyes focused on something behind me. I turned to look, and my breath left my lips in a short gasp.

Ian was there, blocking me from fully enjoying the view like usual, but behind him were the points of the Erast Mountains. Not just the mountains, but a whole city, the gentle glow of a ward surrounding the buildings. The only city along the mountains, aside from Cesa, was

Eraston. It was still night, but the city was thriving. People bustled to and fro, pausing occasionally to look at the strange group we made up. The buildings were modest, but well maintained and clean. The streets held all sorts of vendors, softly speaking to one another as their eyes darted every so often towards us.

Was this what Ian had been hiding from me? A thriving city? Why? I stood, pulling Jonas up with me as I took in my surroundings. A flock of children ran towards us, splitting around Jonas and I to congregate around Ian's tall form.

They were joy incarnate, dirt-streaked faces shining up at Ian. He smiled genially at them, bringing his hand from his pocket full of sweets, remnants of dark magic still swirling from where he'd quickly conjured them. The children crowed, sticky fingers grabbing at Ian's hand as he held it up above their heads, their chattering voices overlapping one another.

"Now, now, we have guests. Can you show some manners and ask nicely?" he cooed at them.

One small girl tilted her head back towards us, rolling her eyes before focusing back on Ian. A chorus of very heartfelt pleases and thank yous had the children scampering away, fists filled with colorful treats.

Ian sauntered towards us, flicking his fingers until a bright red sweet appeared between them with a puff of dark magic. He held it out towards Jonas with a raised brow.

"You almost just passed out. Eat this; it'll make you feel better." The wrapper crinkled as Jonas plucked the sweet from Ian with a murmured thanks, popping it in between his lips. "I know you're probably anxious to get those bracelets off, but I'm sure you two would enjoy a real meal and a soft bed to sleep in first, yes? Follow me." Ian twitched his fingers towards us as he turned, cloak swishing behind him.

I looked to Jonas, who shrugged his shoulders and moved to follow. As we made our way through the winding town, I struggled to reconcile the man in front of us with the man I'd seen in my vision, rising from the corpses of my parents. I would get the story, even if I had to pull every last scrap of magic from Ian's body. Ian was mischief itself, a smile always playing on his lips like he had a secret to tell. He'd had plenty of opportunities to harm me, Avan or Cal, even Jonas, but he'd never acted on it. If a man killed two innocent people in cold blood — unless he was an absolute sociopath — he wouldn't act like this.

There was more to the story, and I wouldn't rest until I had the answers.

Ian stopped in front of a bustling tavern, people mingling on the open porch with drinks and food aplenty. Eyes roamed as conversations hushed, patrons tracking our movements as Jonas, Ian, and I made our way to the bar.

A statuesque woman manned the counter, her eyes tracking our movements with a suspicious expression.

"Good evening, Merri. Three dinners, if you please, an ale for me, and…" Ian trailed off, pointing a finger between Jonas and me with a raised brow. "Are you two even old enough to drink? Water for them."

Any good thoughts I had about him were buried under the bristling anger slicing through me. Jonas was still looking around, not even paying attention to Ian's theatrics.

"Of course, Ian. Your usual table is free." Merri gestured to a small three-seater table in the corner, a small, folded card with a bright star sitting on top. Ian swiped the card as we sat down, flicking and twisting it between his fingers as he observed the bar.

I plopped into the seat across from him, crossing my arms and glaring at the easy way he leaned in the seat. Jonas looked between us before carefully sitting between Ian and me, oblivious to the heat crackling between us. It was a tense and silent few minutes before Merri sat three plates down, ice cold drinks following. Whatever dinner was, it smelled like heaven and my mouth watered at the sight.

Jonas and I dug in like a pair of starved animals, not really caring about the smirk Ian threw our way as he picked at his plate, gently sipping his ale between bites, like the civilized witch he was.

I wiped my mouth, belly full, and finally able to focus without the gnawing hunger of my stomach.

"So, where are we exactly?" I shot towards Ian, hands grasping tight into fists. If he tried anything tricky, he'd get a fistful of magic shoved up his ass.

"Eraston." He shrugged, like that answered everything.

"Obviously; it's the only other city in the mountains," I scoffed.

"That you know of," he replied smoothly.

Interesting. Did he mean there were other witch cities hidden like this? I asked as much, and his laughing non-answer only stoked the fire of my anger.

"I'm not going to give up all my secrets right now, Briar. You'll find out soon enough."

Jonas watched our volleying back and forth like a croquet match as he finished the last of his plate. He cleared his throat, placing his hands together on the table. A soft metallic ring echoed, his bracelets settling gently on his wrists.

"If you two are quite done, I'd like to get these off. Please," he added, almost as an afterthought. Princes probably didn't have to say please very often.

Ian reached a long finger out towards the bracelets, running the pad of his finger over the shiny metal. He contemplated for a moment, the dark glow of his magic briefly illuminating the bracelets before the magic was sucked into the metal. Jonas grit his teeth, flicking his eyes towards Ian with a glower.

"It looks like we can't take them off with magic," Ian murmured.

"Excellent deduction. Shall I call Merri over and the whole bar can celebrate your massive mind?" I drawled.

"If you wouldn't mind, Briar; a celebratory cake would be in order, too, I think. Maybe a kiss, if you're being extra generous," Ian shot back. "Regardless, the only way we're getting these off is the old-fashioned way. The metalsmith doesn't open until morning, so we should get a good night's rest before we meet with him. Isak might not be able to break them if Orin was the one who made them, but he will try."

Jonas nodded at that, gently twisting the bracelets around his wrists with a thoughtful expression. He'd been locked away in that cell by his mother so long ago, did he even remember what his magic felt like? What it was like to dig deep within yourself and simmer in your own powers? I might be new to magic, but the utter loss for just those few days left me aching desperately for the familiar purr of the darkness within me.

We all stood, Ian tossing a small sack of coins on the bar for Merri with a cheeky grin, and we made our way outside. It was chilly now, the looming winter suddenly upon the drafty mountain city. I wrapped my arms around my middle, silently cursing the thin dress I wore. It offered little protection against the soft gusts of wind hitting my body.

It was strange watching Ian interact with the townsfolk. They looked at him with reverence, like he was the savior they had been waiting for. Many people stopped him in the streets, engaging in muted conversations as they peered over his shoulder to look at Jonas and me. What a sight we must have been, thin and dirty from our time in prison.

Warmth circled my shoulders as we walked, and I peered up to Jonas' face, trying to figure out the enigma that he was. We clung together in camaraderie, and I had to wonder if this type of kinship was what held Cal and Avan together like glue.

I still didn't have the full story of their time in that same prison. I barely had anything from them, shuffled from one catastrophe to another in our brief time together. My heart panged at the thought of not knowing where they were, a flush rising in my cheeks at our last interaction. I raised my hand to my chest and rubbed absentmindedly, silently wishing the tug of our bond would flare to life.

Jonas noticed my movements and squeezed me, shooting a soft smile of sympathy my way.

"They'll be fine, Briar. Avan is powerful, even with his magic muted. Cal, well…you know how Cal can be." His lips pursed before twisting into a half smile, looking fondly towards where Ian was striding down the path.

I nudged my shoulder against his, catching his gaze with a raised brow. "You have to tell me that story," I said, wiggling my brows salaciously.

A delicious blush bloomed on Jonas' cheeks as he averted his eyes from mine. "Well, you know the basics. Ian and I met in court, and he was the only one who didn't treat me like a prince. Everyone else simpered and prostrated at the mere sight of me, but Ian? He engaged me in conversations that would make my mother's hair curl." Jonas chuckled, lost in memories. "Everything from war strategies to court gossip, Ian was the bright moment in my long days in the castle. I used to imagine what he was doing when I was in the cell, if he'd started to show his age, if he was still in the capital, working his magic."

Jonas glanced down to his bracelets, twisting his wrist to and fro as light caught the gleam of gold.

"We'll get them off, Jonas. I promise."

"Don't make a promise you can't keep, Briar." Jonas' jaw worked for a moment before he dropped his arm from around me. The aching emptiness he left behind made my heart pang. He caught up to Ian faster than I did, easily integrating himself into the conversation. Jonas' face lit up with a small chuckle, a deep red blooming across his cheeks as Ian touched his shoulder.

Ian turned to look at me, something dark swirling in his gaze. "Come along, Briar. Don't keep us waiting."

"Where's my sister, Ian?" I was getting grumpy and impatient from being dragged all over Alehem, and I ached to know Ainsley and Lucien were safe.

"You can see Ainsley tomorrow. It's late, little bird, and she's probably asleep by now," Ian murmured, striding down the street without a glance back.

I was too tired to argue with him. Something settled in the back of my mind that Ian wouldn't hurt my sister, that she was safe wherever she was. We followed behind Ian like little ducks until he stopped us in front of a modest townhome, one of the larger buildings in the small town. With a flick of his wrist, the door opened to a warm entryway. I could hear the fire crackling in another room, heating the house to a cozy temperature. I poked my head in the rooms as we went by, each one clean and meticulously organized.

"Here we are. I only have one extra room, so you'll have to share. Unless one of you wants to join me?" Ian asked, leaning against the doorjamb with a raised brow.

I rolled my eyes, ignoring the tug of dark longing in my chest, and grabbed Jonas' hand before pulling him behind me into the room. As I made to slam the door in Ian's smug face, he stopped it with his hand, leaning in so close I could smell the mint on his breath.

"No funny business now, little bird. This is my house; you'll play by my rules. I'll know if you've been up to no good."

I stared at him, something burning low in my gut at the dark way he spoke before shaking myself and returning his heated gaze with a sneer.

"You'll have to keep yourself warm tonight, Ian. Bye!" I said, finally closing the door with a slam.

I waved my hands over the door, magic spilling from my fingertips until a shimmering ward encased it. Whirling on Jonas, I grabbed his hands and pulled him to the bed. He threw himself back into the feathery mattress, running his hands along the soft duvet.

"Oh, if Ian is good for one thing, it's this," Jonas sighed, turning his body until his face was pillowed in the blanket. "The man knows how to buy a good mattress." His voice was muffled in the downy fabric, and I shook with laughter as I laid beside him. Ian did, in fact, have the most comfortable mattress I'd probably ever laid on.

We laid silently like that for a few moments, simply enjoying the comfort of a good bed and each other's company. Jonas rolled again, making a pillow for his head out of his arms. He was still too thin, the sharp points of his elbows jutting away from his body, his regal cheekbones hollowed against his face. I smoothed his curls back from where they'd fallen over his brow as he closed his eyes and hummed against my ministrations.

"Jonas…" I whispered.

"Hmm?"

"Is Ian really a bad man?" My voice was small, emotions warring in my chest over the enigmatic man down the hall. A soft, questioning tug filtered through the bond at my thoughts, as if Ian knew we were talking about him.

Jonas opened his eyes halfway, sleep creeping along his consciousness. "Ian's okay. He won't hurt us," he murmured, eyes closing as my fingers ran their path through his hair.

How could I tell him Ian had something to do with my parent's deaths when I had no idea what even happened? Was Ian playing some long game with my life, or was he just some happenstance person involved? Did this have anything to do with the prophecy Avan warned me about?

So many questions, so few answers. I stared out the window, eyes tracking the ascent of the moon until my heavy lids closed of their own accord and sleep took me into its dark embrace.

BRIAR

"You'll take me to see her now, or magic help me, Ian, I'll blow this whole town off the map!"

Ian was lounging in the living room, a leg thrown haphazardly over the back of a plush couch as he flicked through a small book. His gaze bounced to me before refocusing on the words in front of him.

"Ian!" I bellowed.

"Briar!" he shot back. Ian sighed before sitting up, gently closing the book before setting it on the table. "You're awfully grumpy in the mornings. We will see Ainsley after we visit Isak. There are more pressing matters than visiting your perfectly safe sister at…" he glanced at the clock, "nine in the morning. You know she's still sleeping."

Jonas' hands slipped over my shoulders and tugged me gently to face him. I glowered, anger bubbling and rising within me as my magic stretched across my skin. I could feel the fiery anger of Cal's magic simmering just below the surface, itching and begging to be released.

"Don't blow Ian's house up. Please, Briar. I enjoy that bed too much to let it go to waste." Jonas turned his big brown eyes on me, and I couldn't help but melt at the look on his face. To add insult to injury, he held his wrists up between us, gently jangling the bracelets we needed to remove. In my haste to be the only one who mattered, I had forgotten we were meant to visit the metal-smith to try and remove Jonas' bracelets.

Guilt burrowed in my chest as I turned back around to Ian. "You promise right after we see the metal-smith, we will see Ainsley?"

"Cross my heart," Ian said, drawing a small 'x' over his chest. He stopped a step away from me, so close I could see the bloom of his pupils as he looked down at me. It was silent for a beat, tension stretching between us.

"Well...okay. Let's go." I tucked my lower lip between my teeth, gnawing on the soft flesh. Ian's eyes darted to the movement, a dark cloud blossoming behind his eyes as he reached his hand up and tugged my lip from between my teeth.

"Now, now, none of that. Your sister and Lucien are fine. We have to take care of Jonas right now, don't we, little bird?" His voice was soft, my chin still grasped in his warm fingers. I nodded silently as his hand fell away, the coldness he left behind seeping into my heart.

"Well, I can try my best, but no guarantees." Isak was a large man, his head skimming the ceiling of the hot room we stood in. Jonas' encircled wrists were laid out for Isak's perusal against the large anvil in the middle of the room. He kept sneaking glances at me, worry clouding his features.

"Just do what you can, Isak, that's all I can ask for," Ian murmured from where he stood off to the side. His arms crossed tensely across his chest, one finger tapping rhythmically against his bicep. I watched the movement as Isak busied himself with various tools, grabbing a thin chisel and hammer before placing the tip of the tool precariously against the golden bracelet surrounding Jonas' wrist.

"Wait!" I said suddenly, a coil of dread shooting through my chest. "What if there are ward charms in the bracelet? If it breaks, what's to say Ameia or Delani won't know right where to find us?" Panic laced through my chest at the thought of Delani's sharp face as she destroyed the small town looking for us. I was sure they'd noticed our absence by now; Evin couldn't hide that from the Queen forever. I thought he was loyal to the monarchy, but the little quips here and there told me he may have his reservations.

Isak pulled the chisel away, looking at Ian hesitantly. The town was protected by Ian's wards; he was powerful, but would he stand a chance against the might of the crown and council? Ian was silent for a few achingly long minutes, the furrow of his brow deepening with each passing second.

"I need Avan here. Wards and charms are his specialty; he'd probably be able to tell us what exactly is in the bracelet," Ian said.

"Aren't you the one who made the wards surrounding the town? You should be able to determine if there's any wards in the bracelet," I offered.

"The wards surrounding the town are wide sweeping; nothing as delicate as the ones that would be held inside this." Ian gestured to where Jonas stood. He walked to Jonas, contemplating the large gold bands.

I thought back to the warding book in Avan's library, the various small spells and explanations inside. If I could just get my hands on that…

My magic bubbled to the surface, darkness seeping from my hands.

Isak stumbled back, wary eyes darting between me and Ian's stoic face. "Wha-what do you think you're doing?" he shouted.

I closed my eyes, willing my magic out until it caressed Ian's still form, his magic rising to meet mine. Just a small tendril, and I could teleport to Avan's house and...

"Briar." A wall slammed between us, my magic whooshing back to my body. I gasped at the suddenness of it, my eyes popping open to face Ian. "You're scaring Isak. You know, it's not nice to take from others without asking first." Ian raised a brow in my direction, fury coating his features.

"Well, you certainly aren't doing anything to help Jonas!" I snapped, heat rising along my neck.

"You didn't even give him enough time to come up with a plan, Briar," Jonas said softly, moving to stand next to me. "I know your magic is new, but you can't just take Ian's because you want to. What were you trying to use it for?"

"Avan has a warding book at his house. I just thought...maybe it might have something to help us since Avan is..." I choked, the words stuck in my throat. My selfishness was laid bare as the realization of what I'd just done sank in. "I'm sorry. I should've asked," I whispered, turning to Ian.

"You're right. You should have. Don't do it again. Where's the book? I'll retrieve it. You can visit with Ainsley while I'm gone." Ian rose to his full height, the snapping fire of the forge casting his face in shadow as he rounded on me. "Don't take this as my forgiveness, little bird. Remember, my town, my rules. Tell me where the book is."

"In the library, second floor." Shame burned through me as Ian whirled away, his magic crackling in the air. I couldn't believe I'd done that.

It wasn't even a thought to just *take* from Ian. What was wrong with me?

"Thank you, Isak. We'll be back. You two, follow me." Ian's anger was palpable as he stalked from the forge and through the streets. Jonas and I followed wordlessly behind him. I could see Ian's hand clench and release a few times, angry magic weaving in between his fingers with each flex.

"He's really mad," I whispered to Jonas.

"Well, yeah, Briar. You tried to take his magic without his consent. A little communication goes a long way, you know. I'm sure we could've worked something out to get the book instead of you doing your own thing. Your actions affect us all, and you can rely on other people to help. Magic is sacred to witches, and your powers, whatever they may be, pull on the most vulnerable parts of a witch. No one in the history of magic has been able to pull on another's powers with a whim. Even Ameia has the council behind her when she takes magic."

I struggled with that, the vast well of magic inside me even more powerful than the witch queen. Maybe Morina had been right: I should be locked away for everyone's safety.

"I can hear you spiraling from here, Briar. It's…well, it's not okay, but you didn't know. There's so much to learn about the intricacies of being a witch and you can't expect to know them all right away. Ian will forgive you, if you grovel enough." Jonas tossed a wink my way, easing the sting of my actions just a bit.

I sighed, scrubbing the heels of my palms against my eyes as I tried to work through the tangles of shame and anxiety in my chest. Ignorance didn't excuse my actions fully, and Jonas was right. I had to learn to lean on the people around me. Their knowledge and kindnesses would help me navigate the swirling mass of darkness within me.

Quickening my pace, I sidled up to Ian, his green gaze landing on me before glancing away, his jaw clenching tightly.

"What?" he asked, the single syllable striking sharply.

"I wanted to apologize…"

"You already apologized once. Any more apologies are only to soothe yourself," he interrupted.

I nodded, silence stretching between us. As we walked through the empty streets, I thought back to how Avan's apologies felt, his trickery and deceit never really going away no matter how much he prostrated. This was the same. Only a change in actions would really show I was repentant and willing to change.

"Briar!"

My heart leapt in my chest at the familiar halo of blond curls leaning over a house's balcony.

"Ainsley…" I breathed, looking back towards Jonas and over to Ian, who nodded, before running up the steps of the house. I barely took in my surroundings as I bounded up the stairs, my sister's body colliding into mine in the hallway.

Our bodies shook with the force of our combined weeping, only drawing back to study each other's faces. I soothed a hand over Ainsley's cheeks, softly brushing away the tears streaking down them. A quiet mew drew our attention downwards, Lucien purring and weaving between our legs. I scooped him up, burrowing my nose into his orange fur, and cried even more.

"Oh, Briar. It's so good to see you. I've been so anxious about you, and Ian wouldn't tell me anything, other than I had to leave Islar to keep you safe. Is Clarkston okay? Have you seen him? He'll probably be very upset with me for leaving like that, but Ian was so insistent we leave that night. I hope you found my notes. You probably did or you wouldn't be here, but you are! You're safe! Right?" Ainsley's babbling was a balm to my frayed soul.

Ian ascended the stairs behind us, stoic as ever, and that bubbling shame returned to my chest. "Yes, Ian's been very good to me. I'm the one who's been an insufferable bitch." I directed a soft smile towards Ian before focusing back on Ainsley. Lucien jumped from my arms and—the little traitor—padded excitedly towards Ian, who scooped him up in a practiced motion before burying his cheek against Lucien's fur.

"Who's a good boy? Did you miss me?" Ian cooed. My jaw hung open at the sight, Lucien's smug cat face staring back at me. "What?" Ian cocked an eyebrow at me. "I love cats."

Ainsley poured the steaming tea into pretty little cups she brought from the kitchen. I accepted her offer, warming my hands against the porcelain. Jonas was across from me, lounging on the sofa while reading a book. After Ainsley and I got our tears out of the way, Ian bid us farewell, his swirling magic transporting him back to Islar and Avan's house.

I fiddled with the handle, slowly sipping the bergamot concoction Ainsley had brewed, stewing on the emotions in my chest. I missed Avan and Cal terribly, and I gently turned inward to gaze at the fiery red magic twisting with my own. I let a phantom finger trail down the tendril, the magic softly glowing as I did. I let out a deep sigh, drawing the attention of my sister, who was waiting patiently for me to return to the room.

"So, does this mean we go back to Islar?" she asked, a wary look in her eyes. I wasn't sure exactly what Ian had said to make my sister give up the only life she'd known, one that I knew she loved. She just loved me more.

"I don't know, Ains. I don't think so, at least not right now. There's a lot that's happened since I last saw you." I feared telling her about my magic, some small part of me screaming that she was my sister, she wouldn't care, but—

Her eyes moved to Jonas draped across the couch, slightly nodding towards the kitchen for me to follow.

"Spill," she demanded, whirling on me as soon as we crossed the threshold. "I know something is going on, obviously, but you're my sister, Briar. I know when you're hiding things from me. I'm not a child, I can take it."

I cast a nervous glance towards the window, the street outside slowly filling with people as the afternoon wore on. How much had she already seen? Did she know about the people and their magic? About the wards keeping everyone safe?

"Have you seen anything…odd while you've been here?" I ask tentatively.

"Odd?" Her nose wrinkled at the question while she thought. "No, not really? Ian's been very generous to Lucien and me. We haven't wanted for much, and if I needed anything, he got it for me. Why?"

"There's a lot about me you don't know about, that I'm still processing." I heaved in a huge breath, letting it whoosh from my lips in a gust. "I have magic." There. I said it. The words were out in the open with one of the people who meant the most to me in the world, swirling around our heads.

"You do? How?" she asked, leaning against the counter. The soft swish of her dress drew my attention downward, where it would be easier to collect my thoughts. My chest clenched at the thought, and I flicked my eyes back up to Ainsley. Her expression was clear as day, concern written across her features but not distaste or anger. She simply wanted to know.

"I'm not sure if it's a spontaneous mutation, or if Mom and Dad hid something from us, but I'm a witch. I have this magic within me that I'm only just beginning to scratch the surface of understanding. Avan…" My words caught in my throat, a choking sound the only thing coming from my mouth as I thought about his deceit, his careful words, the way his hands roamed my body, that cheeky smile, his dishonesty about my magic.

"He was the one who took you from Islar, right?" Ainsley prodded gently. I nodded, words still escaping me as the enormity of everything crashed down within me. Did Cal know about Avan's secrets? Were they in on it together? His magic roiled within me, roaring at my distress.

"He, um, he's the one who taught me about my magic before we were separated. Apparently, my magic is very powerful, and the crown took notice of me. In witch society, at a certain age, you must register with the crown." I left out the bit about Ameia taking bits of witches' magic. I still needed to talk with Jonas about that. "My magic rejected it. So, I had three witch trials I needed to complete while Avan and Cal were kept away from me."

"Cal?" Ainsley prompted, dragging the teapot close and bringing down two more delicate cups from the nearby cabinet. The steam helped clear the tears threatening to spill from my eyes as I accepted the tea from her hands. "Tell me more about him. Avan, too. They seem very dear to you."

"I barely know them," I whispered into my cup, afraid the words would steal the little sliver of Cal's magic I'd hoarded.

"That doesn't mean anything, Briar. Mom and Dad only knew each other for a few months before they married and had you, don't you remember? They were so happy. Your eyes light up when you say Avan and Cal's names; they must be special to have captured your heart." She placed a gentle hand against mine, squeezing softly.

"They are special, but they've also hurt me, with their words and inactions, with their *lies*." I hissed out the last word, biting through my teeth. Tears sprang unbidden in my eyes, angry, harsh tears that threatened to spill down my face. I swiped at my eyes, unwilling to shed another tear over those pompous asses.

"Avan lied to me. He said he didn't know the type of magic I carried. I don't know if Cal did, and I'm not sure if I want to. The Queen imprisoned them both during my trials, and now? I don't even know where they are." I explained our bond, how Ian's meddling had somehow amplified it between Avan and me, how the golden ties still strung us together after breaking his spell. A mysterious winter tang filled my nose as I spoke about the bond, my magic wrapping delicately around the questioning tug. There were so many things I didn't understand about the bond, including where it came from and how it impacted my relationships.

"So, even with this bond, you can't figure out where they are now?" Ainsley prompted, refilling our cups.

I shook my head, "The Queen muted our magic with handcuffs. I assume they still have them on because I can't feel them." I rubbed a hand absently against the place in my chest usually occupied by the warm ember of Cal and springy sweetness of Avan. "I assume they can only be removed by a council member; I fear there may be charms or enchantments that prevent just anyone from cutting them off."

"That is quite the conundrum. Is that what's on your friend's wrists?" Her eyes darted to the other room, a peek of Jonas' feet visible through the open door. I nodded at her, filling the contemplative silence with a sip of tea.

"Can't you take them off? You say you have this powerful magic, moreso than your Avan or Ian, so why wouldn't you be able to?" Ainsley took a step towards me, grasping my hand in hers.

"She should. With this." Ian appeared in the kitchen, windblown hair in disarray and Avan's warding book clutched in his hand. "Hello, little bird. Miss me?"

BRIAR

We spent most of the afternoon pouring through Avan's warding book, looking at his scribbled annotations for the most intricate spells. I was wary of my magic enough to take pause and fully absorb his written tutelage, running my finger over the indented pages. He was hurried in his script, slanted letters and messy scribbles showing his mind moving much faster than his hand.

I landed on one promising spell, a tricky one meant to destabilize a ward long enough to break through. I thought if I was able to tweak it and hold the spell, Isak could smash the bracelet without triggering any potential countercharms.

"Look at this." I offered the book to Ian, pointing at the spell I'd just found. I quickly explained it to him, tossing my hand over the book as I did.

"Interesting," Ian mumbled, taking the book from my proffered hands and running an elegant finger down the page. I swallowed at the gesture, his face scrunched in thought as he ran his other hand absently through his curls. His hair had grown, curling in on itself, and his hand created a soft halo of mussed curls with each pass. His gaze flicked to me, wholly focused on my face while he worked his jaw. "This might just work. Good job, little bird."

A bloom of heat wove through my chest at his praise, our shoulders touching as he sidled up next to me, explaining the more abstract concepts of the spell. I had so much I needed to ask him, and his nearness wasn't helping me form the words.

"Once I saw the spell and its components, it all became clear. Like I said before, I have a broad understanding of wards, but it's the breakdowns of the spells I have trouble with. See, here, the amalgamation of the individual spells creates the ward; it's layer upon layer of weaving magic. Amazing," Ian breathed, his excitement shining through as he gazed at me, our shoulders touching as we looked at each other over the open book.

Distrust certainly didn't equal distaste as I took in his handsome face, harsh lines tempered by the excitement of learning. I felt that heat from my chest work its way down through my stomach, settling into my core the longer we stared at each other. Ian's lips were plump, spreading apart as if he wanted to say something more. The bond flared to life between us, dragging our bodies unconsciously closer together, our breaths mingling, eyes locked together.

My heart thumped in my chest as I leaned in towards him, our noses barely brushing, only a few more inches and…

"Briar!" Jonas slammed the door shut behind him, making Ian and I jump apart. My blood pounded in my head as a blush rose against my cheeks. Ian's skin flushed as well, and it gave me soft comfort knowing

I wasn't the only one affected.

"Please, for the love of magic, tell me you found something." Jonas flopped dramatically against the couch, flinging his arm over his face. The longer he was away from those dungeons and the more food he had in his stomach, the more his playful personality shone. His face was losing that sharp edge of hunger and he was gaining a little bit of weight back.

I cleared my throat, moving to kneel next to Jonas to show him the passage I found. I glanced up one last time to Ian, finding his burning gaze on me, something dark promised there.

"Um, yes, I did. Look here, at this passage." I pointed to the correct paragraph, explaining the details and what we would need Jonas to do in order to make sure the destabilizing spell worked correctly. He would need to hold absolutely still while Isak, Ian, and I worked. His eyes glazed over halfway through my explanation before he waved me off.

"Warding spells are boring, Briar, and I trust you and Ian know what you're talking about. Can we go?" he said, springing up from the couch and grabbing mine and Ian's hands before dragging us from the townhome. I waved at Ainsley on our way out, promising to be back soon. She waggled her eyebrows at me, glancing to where I was sandwiched between Jonas and Ian. My cheeks burned again at her implications, so I stuck my tongue out at her before the door closed behind us.

Jonas took us down the street, his body practically vibrating with excitement before Ian pulled against my hand, stopping us in the road.

"It's that way." Ian pointed a finger in the opposite direction, raising his brow at Jonas, who promptly turned us around and all but ran.

The fire crackled merrily in Isak's shop, and he took a small step back with a raised brow as Jonas pulled us to a stop.

"Briar thinks she'll be able to remove any warding so you can cut the bracelet off!" Jonas said excitedly, letting go of my hand to wave the bracelets in front of Isak's shocked face. Isak pursed his lips and nodded, ushering us into the forge and positioning Jonas' wrists on his anvil.

"You better be right about this, young lady," Isak rumbled at me. "Wouldn't want to bring the council down on our necks." He settled the chisel against Jonas' bracelets, nodding at me to begin.

I glanced at Ian, his gaze on Jonas instead of me, calculation in his eyes. Sighing, I looked inward, gently teasing my magic to bend to my will. I murmured the incantation, dark smoke slowly leaking from my fingertips to buzz and prod at the bracelets. There was a wall there, the wards I expected. Breathing through my nose, I called up a mental image of the book, working through each ward until a fuzzy haze surrounded Jonas' wrists. He huffed a breath, the only noise aside from my words and the crackling fire of the forge.

"Now, Isak," Ian chimed in, and Isak brought the hammer down against the chisel, snapping the bracelet on Jonas' right wrist clean in half. The wards screamed against the intrusion, the siren charms warring against my destabilizing spell. Jonas huffed but held still as Isak set the chisel against Jonas' left wrist and repeated the action.

With a whirl of screaming magic, the bracelets wards disintegrated under my ministrations, floating away into the air. Ian stepped in, wrapping his own dark magic around the broken spells before they could reform, tossing the smoky ball into the hot forge. I could almost hear the screams of the spells as the ball fell apart in the flames.

"Holy shit, it worked," Jonas breathed, bringing his wrists to eye level before whooping and rushing out to the street. He ran to the fountain across from Isak's shop, icy blue magic streaming from his hands. Large animals made of water galloped from the fountain, prancing around the top of the spout before collapsing. I ran out to meet him, his huffing form bent over as he caught his breath.

"It's been decades since I've used my magic, I'm a bit out of practice." He grinned up at me. Jonas stood, sobering quickly as he enveloped me in a hug. "Thank you, Briar," he murmured against my hair. I soothed a hand up and down his back, letting him have all the time in the world. My magic glowed within me, a new soft tug pulling at my chest, the sweet bloom of winter berries exploding on my tongue. We separated, simply staring at one another in amazement before Ian's gentle cough caused us to jump apart. Jonas' hand stayed twisted in mine, though, the warmth that hadn't left from this morning still curling low in my stomach.

"There is still so much I don't know about my magic, though. Please, Ian!" I turned my most pathetic look on him, widening my eyes and pouting my lips. He had the most stupendous library in his townhome, and he insisted we make dinner before he let me loose within the stacks.

Jonas and Ainsley were at the market, night now fully descended on Eraston, and the town had come alive. I learned the night witches here flourished in the darkness, drawing their powers from the moonlight.

Ian worked his own magic, whipping a creamy mixture in the bowl in front of him, a levitating tomato chopped by a sharp knife next to him while a grater ran across a lemon on the counter. I was in charge of boiling the noodles, and to be quite honest, he could probably do that himself while I looked at the books.

"This will go much faster with the two of us working together, little bird," Ian chirped cheerfully, a joyful expression on his face. He waved a hand, causing the tomato and lemon zest to mix in with his sauce, and he dipped the spoon in before tasting it. "Delicious. Would you like to try?" He offered the spoon my way, and I couldn't say no. The acidity of the tomato and lemon mixed with whatever sauce he had created filled the kitchen with its spicy aroma.

I stepped closer, opening my mouth for him to ladle the mixture into. His eyes bored into mine as he tipped the spoon forward, lemony garlic bursting across my tongue. I groaned, tipping my head back and closing my eyes as I enjoyed the taste. My eyes opened to Ian staring at me like he was a starving man in the desert. Warmth bloomed in my chest as his affectionate tug on the bond twirled around me.

"That is really good, Ian," I murmured.

"It should be, I made it," he replied, a snort and raised eyebrow tossed my way.

I placed my hands against my hips, a smart retort bubbling to the surface before Ian stepped forward, crowding my space.

"I like that look on your face, little bird. When you silently tell me to fuck off, it makes me want to bend you over this counter and show you exactly what I want to do to that smart mouth of yours." His gaze was hooded as he stared down at me.

I should be furious, but the throbbing low in my core said otherwise. His arms bracketed me against the counter as he ran his nose up the column of my throat. I forced my shaking hands to clench at my sides, resisting the urge to thread them through Ian's dark locks.

"Tell me you don't want this as badly as I do, Briar, and I'll stop," he murmured into my ear. My breath caught in my throat. Did I want him to stop? I should push him away, still not knowing what part he played in my parent's deaths…but really? I didn't, couldn't. The way he doted on the children of the village, how patient he was with Jonas and me invading his space, how he protected Ainsley and Lucien from the council, the way I sometimes caught his eyes tracking me…

I tell myself I should hate him; deep, burning, all-consuming hatred. Instead, the burn I feel isn't hate, but how thin is that line? Between love and hate?

No. I didn't hate Ian. At all.

"If you don't tell me to stop, I'm going to lose this last thread of control I have. You'd like that, wouldn't you, little bird?" I couldn't bring myself to disagree with him. Instead, my gaze shot to his and I nodded. I saw him break, the star-flecked darkness in his eyes flaring bright before he slammed his mouth against mine. This wasn't going to be gentle, our mouths forming together with furious teeth and tongues. He still hadn't fully forgiven me for trying to take his magic, but the simmering lust thrown down the bond told me exactly how he felt in this moment.

Our hands grasped at each other's clothing, dinner all but forgotten as Ian flicked a hand towards the pot bubbling on the fire, moving it away from the flames. He lifted me onto the counter, buttons snapping and flying as he ripped my dress clean down the middle. Ian mouthed along my jaw and down the column of my throat as my hands threaded through his curls. He slipped my dress over the curve of my shoulder, parting the fabric until I was exposed to the warm kitchen air.

Ian nipped and bit along my chest, leaving bruising marks in his wake

I was sure to feel for days. His hands gripped my hips tightly, bunching the fabric of my dress as he rutted against me, only a few layers of fabric separating us. Heat pooled in my stomach as I jumped over that line, blooming lust planting itself firmly within me. His mouth moved to my breast, his tongue lapping and sucking until he left me a sobbing mess on the counter.

My hands scrambled against his shirt, ripping buttons until his dark curls peeked out at me. I ran my hands along his chest, pulling his face to mine as we met in a blistering crash. Ian's chest pushed me back until I was spread like a feast on the wooden countertop, his fingers dipping below the gathering of my skirts to gather the wetness pooling between my legs. He circled me, agonizingly slow and not at all the furious pace we'd set initially.

"This is in the way," he grinned, grasping the ruined dress in his fists and pulling until the fabric fell away underneath me. My chest heaved as I gazed down at Ian's tall form drinking me in, thoroughly enjoying the way his pupils blew until nothing but a rim of green was visible amidst the black. His hands threaded through mine, and he leaned forward until the stretch in my shoulders gave way, gently trapping my wrists against the edge of the counter. "Don't move these, little bird."

"Or what?" My retort was more breathy than snappy, and Ian's handsome face filled my view as his gaze caught mine. His deft fingers had stirred a rebellious heat within me, and I could feel myself getting fidgety that he hadn't continued.

"Do you want me to make good on my promise and fuck you on the edge of the counter? Or shall I leave you breathless and wanting, naked here until you learn my rules do indeed have consequences?" He sketched a brow at me, content to wait for my answer.

I rolled my eyes and was rewarded with a swift pluck of my nipple from the same fingers that had stirred up this agonizing heat.

"Tick, tock, Briar. I could go back to making dinner, or…" I cut him off with a nipping kiss, slapping my hands against the counter with a huff.

"That's my girl."

Infuriating man.

His nose grazed down my chest, eyes peeking up at me as he nipped and licked slowly at the juncture of my thighs and hips, my breath wavering as I fought to keep my eyes on him. My hands shook where they gripped the edge of the counter, more from impatience than actual effort.

"Ian, magic above, please…" The words died on my tongue as he finally gave in, firmly grasping my hips as his tongue speared me. I groaned into my shoulder, unable to keep my eyes open while he licked and sucked and nipped at every intimate part of me. Ian's nose nuzzled at my bundle of nerves while his tongue nudged at me, zapping sensations working their way through my core. All the while, I hung on, panting, desperate to find out how I'd be rewarded for my good behavior.

I came with a garbled shout, my hips rising as Ian continued to work me through the aftershocks. My magic whirled within me, threatening to spill from my fingertips, but I tamped it down, wanting to watch as Ian lapped at me gently. I found a little bit of that star-flecked night in his gaze, wholly focused on me as he rose from his kneeling position. The bond was warm between us, and I could feel the ties pulling tighter, cementing it into place.

Ian tapped my hip, gently encouraging me to twist until my chest was flush against the counter. My hands remained firmly grasping at the edge as his hand grazed my back and down the swell of my ass. His fingers dipped inside me, gathering my arousal and spreading it around my sensitive nub excruciatingly slow. Without any warning, Ian plunged inside of me, his cock a deliciously intrusive stretch.

My forehead met the counter with a loud groan from my lips, Ian's hands gripping my hips as he set a bruising pace. Bottles and bowls rattled around me as our hips slapped together, our breaths rushing in synchrony that echoed around the kitchen.

His hand left my hip and snaked around my chest, pulling me up and flush against him. His hand wove around my throat, squeezing gently, while the other kneaded at my aching breasts.

"You take my cock so well, little bird. Such a good listener. You deserve to be rewarded, don't you?" he murmured in my ear. I nodded fervently, gasping as he tweaked my nipple with his fingers, each pluck sending a zap straight to my core. "Do you deserve to come again?"

"Please, Ian, yes, please!" I whined, spurred on by the sensations working their way through my body. His pace wasn't fast enough to create the friction I needed, my breasts aching and tight, that simmering heat just low enough not to boil over into what I chased. He slowed his thrusts, each agonizing pull making me gasp and moan in frustration.

"Tell me what you need, little bird," Ian whispered in my ear, sending a shiver throughout my body.

"Faster, please. You promised!" I gasped out, magic slowly seeping from my fingertips. A starry night began to whirl around us, churning faster with each breathy gasp that left my mouth. The bond flared to life, and I could sense those golden ties between us with each thrust of Ian's hips.

"I did indeed, and you've been such a good little bird for me. Now, tell me whose sweet pussy this is, and I'll let you come." Ian's hand dropped from my throat, tapping gently against my clit as he waited for my answer.

"Ohhh, it's yours Ian, please, oh!" His answering chuckle in my ear was the only warning I got before he pressed me firmly back against the counter, Ian's hand pressing into my back to create an arch that had his cock hitting just the right spot inside of me. Ian set a furious pace, my nipples dragging against the counter as bottles rolled off, my hands holding onto the edge in front of me until my knuckles were white from the strain.

Ian finally lost control, grunting and panting along with each thrust, his careful mask finally falling as I turned my face to look at him. He stared down at where we were joined, watching himself plunge in and out of me, a look of rapture on his face. He caught my gaze and smirked, dragging his hand from my hip to crack across my ass, redness blooming on the tender skin. Ian rubbed at it gently before delivering another satisfying smack across the other cheek. I couldn't hold it in any longer; the mingling sensations, along with the settling of the bond between us lighting up every nerve in my body as I soared higher and higher, was enough to drive me crazy.

An explosion of stars and darkness surrounded us as we came together, his magic and mine whirling in unison with our combined release, the golden ties planting themselves firmly within my chest. I panted against the counter, my cheek pressed into the grain so hard, I was sure it was going to leave an imprint. Ian crowded my back, his heavy breathing matching my own. His hands slid up and down my back, his mouth pressing soft kisses against my skin before he pulled from me fully, our combined release dripping down my thighs.

"Are you okay?" Ian asked as he turned my jelly-like body over, bundling me into his arms. My ass rested against the counter while his hands soothed down my back and sides, working some of the knots he found along my spine.

"M'okay," I mumbled against his shoulder as my eyes drooped.

Ian gently grabbed my chin in his fingers, drawing my gaze up to meet his. He placed a soft kiss against the tip of my nose before helping me stand on wobbly legs. "Go take a bath and get some sleep. I'll finish dinner, and tomorrow, we can look at the library."

I pouted a little, wanting him to join me in the soapy water, but Jonas and Ainsley would be back soon. They probably wouldn't want to eat dinner if they walked in on our naked forms in the kitchen. Nodding, I reached my lips for a sipping kiss from Ian before he turned me around, slapping my ass to shoo me from the kitchen. I glared at him, bending to grab my torn dress and squealing from the room when he stepped closer.

"You'll have to be faster than that!" I shouted, all but sprinting from the kitchen as he chased me up the stairs.

Maybe a bubbly second round wasn't completely out of the question.

BRIAR

Another portion of my good behavior was access—finally—to Ian's vast library. It didn't hold a candle to the citadel library, but I was ravenous for the information inside nonetheless. Maybe between the silent stacks, I could pull more information from Ian. He was behind me, silently munching on a mysterious purple fruit, running his hand over the spines stacked neatly on the shelves.

Where Avan's library was organized chaos, Ian's was meticulous. Each shelf was dusted religiously, books stacked and categorized in a system only Ian knew. The books were all aligned—probably magicked to be the same size, while creating a uniform and pleasing display.

"Do you have anything about meta witches?" I asked tentatively, not sure if I would like what I found. Ian hummed, tilting his head side to side before snapping his fingers and beckoning me to follow. The library wove underneath his townhome, somehow magically spanning three floors below the earth. I jogged to keep up, passing by lit sconces that threw his face into sharp relief as he strode by. "I actually wanted to ask you something…"

He turned into a darkened alcove, twisting and advancing on me with a predatory gaze. Ian's lips twisted up before he grasped my chin firmly and brought my lips to his. We fought for dominance, our tongues clashing against each other as he backed me into a shelf. His fingers laced with mine, bringing my arms up above my head before trapping my wrists in his strong grip. Ian rucked my skirts up, his fingers sliding inside me easily, his moan against my mouth the most delicious sound.

"You're so wet for me already, little bird." Ian's lips moved against mine before pressing back, his fingers curling inside of me. "You looked so beautiful standing amongst the books, I couldn't help myself. I need to hear you screaming my name in these stacks or I'll go absolutely mad."

"You just wanted to distract me from my—ah!—questions." My head thunked back against the shelf as Ian hit a particularly good spot, massaging his fingers back and forth before he brought his thumb up to circle my clit. "Ah, yes, yes, yes, yes!"

Ian's free hand tugged the neck of my dress down—leaving my hands right where he left them—the stretchy fabric allowing him to free one of my breasts to tweak and knead. His kisses moved from my lips to my jaw and down my throat before nibbling on the lobe of my ear. I was a myriad of sensations, everywhere he touched lighting up, the tug between our chests releasing a pleasant thrum as Ian worked my body with his skilled fingers.

"That's not true, Briar. You look so adorable when you read; your nose gets all crinkled and your eyebrows pull together when you come to a particularly interesting passage. I couldn't help but watch you, and then I started thinking about you coming around my cock as I fucked you against the shelf, and, well, I just couldn't help myself when you asked for my assistance." His fingers withdrew with a soft smack before he brought them to his mouth, sucking on the glistening digits as his eyes rolled back at the taste. "Perfection."

I brought my hands down to fiddle with the buttons on his pants, but Ian ruined my fun by bundling my wrists in his hands. "Ah, ah, little bird. You had a question?" He sketched a brow at me, lips curling into a devious smile. "Would you like to make a deal?"

"I don't want a deal, Ian. I want you to fuck me against this bookshelf like you promised." I pouted as Ian chuckled, his fingers tapping against my lips.

"All in good time. Ask your question first and I'll tell you where the lineage books are."

"Not fair."

"Entirely fair. We both get something we want. Time is ticking."

I sighed, the heat in my stomach suddenly turning sour. I liked the direction Ian and I had been heading and this was going to be difficult to talk about. I heaved a breath and side-stepped to give myself a bit of air before I began.

"My last trial, they gave me a potion, something that threw me back in time. The council said it was to test my emotions, how I would react to a distressing situation." I worried my nail between my teeth, biting and pulling at the skin until I could taste copper. Ian furrowed his brows, grasping my hand to pull it away from my biting. "It was the night my parents died."

His eyes darkened, and I couldn't help but wonder if he remembered exactly what I was talking about.

"My sister and I were there, you know, when they died. I didn't remember what happened for the longest time; everything was so hazy and messy. Whatever they gave me put everything into crystal clear focus. I saw their faces. I'd forgotten what they'd looked like..." I trailed off, eyes unfocused as I dived back into the memories. Ian, thankfully, stayed quiet, even when my hand twitched in his. "They were going to run from something. They said someone was going to help them escape..."

Ian started at that, his gaze sharpening. "Your family lived in Islar your whole life, Briar? You didn't move there from the capital?" His voice was low, and time slowed for just a moment.

"You were there, too, you know. I'm sure you remember that. You made me forget, though," I murmured.

"No, no, no, little bird, listen to me. Everything makes so much sense now. Please just listen to what I have to say before you make any decisions." His face swam in my watery vision, and I barely had a hold on the magic within me. Cal's fire burned through my veins, begging me to tear the entire library down, Ian included. He wasn't trying to deny it; he just wanted me to listen. I didn't know if I could move, even if I wanted to. A soft tug from his end of the bond brought me back to the moment as his eyes fixed on mine.

He sighed, his chin meeting his chest before his gaze rose back up. Both of Ian's hands twined around mine and I could feel his magic tickling along the bond between us, soothing and wrapping around me to temper the raging inferno I felt.

"You know about the prophecy?" Ian asked quietly. I nodded mutely. "The council found out about Avan's plans, how he wanted to destroy the object he sought. Delani learned of his plans and worked with the council to supersede his actions. She wanted whatever it was the fortune teller was talking about, always hungry for more power. She and Orin crafted a bigger version of the spell Avan had worked, finding an imprecise location of a family of witches living in a small town along the Sirith river: Islar."

Ian's eyes widened at me, begging me to listen for just a moment longer. "My parents?"

"Yes, and you and Ainsley, although we didn't know it at the time. I worked as hard as I could to tell them without causing alarm within the council. I wanted to protect this small family, but I also have my own people to think of. I couldn't throw out everything I'd worked towards for Eraston to alert the council that I knew about their plans. Plus, I had Avan to contend with." He chuckled humorlessly, and I knew how stubborn Avan was. I couldn't imagine him with the youthful crown of ignorance upon his head, too.

"Their spell was set to go off that night, to destroy your family and any resistance that Delani thought might come to the crown someday. I was able to get a missive to your parents, to hide, but when I arrived at the house and found them…I knew I was too late." His voice cracked at the last part, pure torture in his eyes. "I thought the entire family was gone, that Delani had succeeded in her insane plan, but then a little girl emerged from the back door, big grey eyes taking in the scene, and I knew I had to protect her as fiercely as I had failed to protect her parents. So, I worked a memory charm, to erase any memories of magic she might have seen, anything she might've remembered about that night."

I fell to my knees, Ian following me to the floor. "You tried to save us? It wasn't Avan's spell?" He nodded at me, eyes searching mine.

"What happened to Delani? And Orin?" Surely, the death of two witches wouldn't go unnoticed by the Queen.

Ian's mouth opened and closed a few times, furious anger blooming behind his eyes. "Nothing," he said tersely. "Nothing, and no one could do anything about it. Avan and Cal were sent to the dungeons, Jonas locked up, and I—"

"Did what you could to save your people," I finished for him. He swallowed, working his jaw. I reached up to run my fingers along the feathering muscle, smoothing along his face until my fingers tangled in his hair. My lips pressed softly to his, our shared past comforting each other.

"I had no idea it was you in that dress shop, Briar. I swear to the magic above I didn't know," he murmured. "You simply called to me. I hadn't set foot in Islar since that night, but something called me, pulled me there, and when I saw your face, I couldn't help myself."

It was silent for a beat, our chests moving in sync as we sat on the cold stone, content in the silence.

Ian cleared his throat, wide eyes gazing down at me before he made to stand. "I am truly sorry for how it all turned out," he murmured, bringing my body close to him in a gentle embrace.

"I forgive you. Who knows what would have happened if my magic had manifested by itself in Islar?" I shuddered, imagining the horror Islardians would've wreaked upon my little family.

"Speaking of your magic." Ian straightened. "We have a book to find."

I smiled softly and whirled from his embrace, grabbing a sconce from where it hung on the wall and dragging it along with me to light the way. My fingers ran down the spines as I searched, turning over Ian's words in my mind. As I walked, I toyed with my magic, stretching and flexing it like a muscle. Cal's warm orange intertwined with mine, mixing and twisting. Ian left me to my devices, staying behind in the hallway, and now that I was alone with my thoughts, a deep ache settled in my chest.

Where were Avan and Cal? Were they okay? The only flickering in the bond I felt was from Ian, their golden ties disappearing into the void. There was the faint kiss of winter I felt every so often, but I wasn't sure exactly what that was. It could be Jonas, but we hadn't explored anything beyond companionship, let alone a bond. Avan and Cal hadn't appeared in my dreams, either from lack of my magic reaching out to them or…

I didn't want to think about what the other possibility could be.

I plucked and pulled at various books, attempting to distract my train of thought and focus on the task at hand. Nothing gave me the answers I was looking for, or only mentioned meta witches in passing.

Something caught my eye, glinting in the firelight. There sat a gold flecked book, the edges so worn that even the title was missing. A pang in my chest drew me towards it, my fingers softly running along the spine before taking it fully off the shelf. I slid down the wall, landing in a puff of skirts and small dust motes.

Flicking to the front page, I traced the words *A Brief History of Meta Witchery and its Magical Practices* and slowly turned the page, beginning to read.

"From the word 'meta', witches containing this power are those connected most to the manna of magic. All that is, all that was, all that will be. Meta witches are the rarest of us all, destined to be leaders. Whether good or bad is up to the individual magic user."

I sat back, absorbing the words. Avan had simply named my powers to the Queen, and I had so many questions swirling in my brain about what that actually meant. 'All that is, all that was, all that will be.' The magic inside me was connected to manna, the book says, but what is manna? I looked back to the book, devouring the words inside.

"Manna is defined as the magic that permeates all, seeping deep into the earth, absorbed high into the skies above. All living beings possess manna, and witchery in general harnesses the potent magic and bends it to the witch's selected skill. For example, a water elemental witch connects most with liquid magic, pulling gaseous water from the air. Some witches possess a duality—an elemental and telepathic nature, for example. Meta witches, however, have the elastic capability to harness manna at its most base level, able to create any and all magic, connect with magical beings, and mold the manna into any inclination."

Ian found me a few moments later, all thoughts of his promises flying out the window with the look I shot him.

"Here," I said simply, handing the book over. His eyes darted quickly as he flipped through the pages, running a hand over his mouth as he sat back on his haunches. Ian flicked his gaze to me once he was done, a similar awestruck look on his face that I was sure mirrored my own.

"This is…unbelievable," he murmured. "So, this connection? You can control it? You can control the manna itself? Think of the implications here, Briar!"

"That's it, though. I don't have control over it! I didn't even know there was a bond until you showed up, and what about when my magic explodes? What if I hurt someone? Or unknowingly use my magic to manipulate them? Maybe the council was right and I am dangerous." I gnawed on my lip as anxiety rose with every question that poured from my mouth. I couldn't imagine thinking I had unwillingly roped Avan, Cal, and Ian into this bond we shared, and what about Jonas?

"Hey, hey," Ian said, dropping the book and grabbing my face in his hands. "You are no danger. You do have control, and you must remember you just found out about magic, about witches. You will grow, and learn, and love, and everything good that comes with being a witch. The fact that you learned of your powers doesn't negate the years you've already lived. You know who you are as a person, and would that person consider themselves a danger?"

I shook my head, letting the words sink in, Ian gently nudging me from the hole I'd let myself fall into. I leaned into his side, his arms twining around me and pulling me close. Ian's peppery scent filled my nose, and I buried my face into his chest while his arms rubbed soothing circles on my back.

"You do know what this means, don't you?" Ian said softly.

"No," I mumbled into his chest.

"I get to train you." I could hear the devilish glee in his voice, and as I looked up into his emerald stare, the joy in his face caused me to giggle softly. "If you listen and do your homework, maybe you'll earn a reward, hmm?"

Now *that* was a plan I could get behind.

"Shush, I'm concentrating," Jonas chastised Ainsley and me, his hands carefully placing a card at the top of the tower he'd built.

Our conversation continued despite Jonas' attempts at complete silence—as if the wind from our voices could knock his project over.

"There's dancing and music, and *food*, Briar. I think I even saw a pastry stall." Ainsley wiggled her eyebrows at me. "Please come with me! You'll have so much fun, I promise!"

Apparently, each evening, the night witches celebrated their moon goddess, Alwyn, praying for peace and serenity under her watchful gaze. The town lit up at night, preferring to handle its business after dark. Stalls along the main street opened, offering various goods and services to the townsfolk. Some transplants still operated during the day, but they were few and far between, as most residents were born and raised night witches.

I hummed, gently threading my fingers into hers, snuggling against her warm side. "I don't know, Ains…"

"I bet you could get Ian or Jonas to dance with you," she whispered conspiratorially in my ear. "Jonas keeps sneaking looks at you when he thinks no one's looking."

I peeked over her shoulder at the man intently working on his card tower. He'd been filling out quite nicely since we arrived, his already handsome face losing some of that sharpness he'd accumulated in the dungeons.

"Jonas doesn't feel that way about me, Ainsley," I whispered back to her, ignoring that icy sharp tug in my chest that said otherwise. I wasn't one hundred percent sure the winter magic belonged to Jonas, and it would be silly of me to assume. He had gone through decades of being alone without his magic; Jonas needed to relearn how to be himself before aligning with some girl he'd just met.

"You should come with us, Briar. Ainsley is right; it is quite fun." Jonas turned to us, grinning and flourishing his hands at the tower. By doing so, however, he created a great gust of air, toppling his hard work.

Ainsley and I cackled at the heartbroken look on his face before I agreed, if only to make him feel better.

To be honest, when we arrived later that night to the town square, it was quite enjoyable. Glimmering string lights filled with bright magic hung across the town square that slowly filled with people the more the night went on.

Ainsley and I filled our baskets with various goods, sneaky treats to bring back to Ian's house and trinkets I couldn't tear my eyes from. A tinkling brass dancer sat suspended in my palm as we sat on the edge of the festivities. He twirled sinuously in the air, small metal hands weaving around each other as his legs sprang up and landed on my skin. My sister leaned in, her bright blue eyes wide and focused on the small treat of magic.

"That's amazing!" she breathed, leaning in closer and gently tipping my hand until the dancer sprang into her palm. His dance changed, something lighter and reminiscent of spring and life. She ooo-ed and ahh-ed, her distraction allowing me to watch the people slowly leaking into the town square.

A band started a jaunty tune from somewhere off to the side, and, in perfectly practiced synchronization, people began moving with each other. The song was loud and fast, giggling couples twirling in the dirt in front of us. I watched with rapt attention, quickly memorizing the fast steps. We had a few festivals in Islar, but nothing as joyous as this. People were having fun.

Their inhibitions flew into the night sky as the taste of magic bloomed in the air. Ainsley stirred next to me, gently tucking the brass dancer into her basket before turning her attention on the growing haze of magic. Sparks flew from the spinning dancers, leaping into the sky before being sucked into the dark night air. Ainsley's eyes tracked the dancers, her hands fidgeting with the skirt of her dress as she itched to join them.

"Would you want to dance with me?" I leaned into her, shouting to be heard above the merriment. She nodded furiously, our baskets forgotten on the edge of the circle as we linked our hands together and spun into the vortex of bodies.

Ainsley whooped and hollered as we spun, twisting against me before spinning away into the arms of someone else. The band picked up the pace, our pounding feet stamping into the dirt, trying desperately to keep up. Ainsley spun back into me, her bubbling laughter infecting me until I could hardly contain my joy.

My magic itched to leak out with so much magic surrounding us until my skin felt prickly and hot. Thankfully, the band slowed, leaving a mass of panting bodies and soft clapping. Their next tune was slower and more deliberate, weeding out most of the dancers until only a few couples remained, entwined in each other's arms as they swayed slowly to the beat. I grabbed Ainsley's hand and dragged her back to our spot, where Ian and Jonas had finally joined us.

Ian raised a brow at our sweaty, grinning forms as Ainsley and I plopped onto the bench next to him.

"Aw, I wanted to dance!" Jonas whined, looking wistfully at the slow-turning couples still in the square. He turned and locked eyes with me, something unreadable in his gaze. "Would you twirl around with me, Briar? I know all the good court dances, and I promise I won't step on your toes."

I sighed, tipping my head back against the bench and shooting a grin his way. Ian nudged my side, and as I turned to him, he smiled softly and mouthed at me to go. I turned back to Jonas, slapping my hand into his outstretched one as he pulled me towards him, beginning to spin slowly in time with the song.

It was nice, enjoying the evening with them, and I sank into Jonas' embrace, just focusing on the music and how his warm hands held mine.

"You look very pretty tonight," he murmured as I looked up at him, admiring the soft dimple in his chin that only appeared when he smiled.

"I'm glad you bullied me into coming out. I needed a night off," I said, leaning my head against his chest. His breaths were almost in time with the soft plucks of the music, and it helped to clear my mind of the ever-present swirling thoughts.

"It wasn't bullying, sweetheart. It was gentle encouragement." He chuckled, the laugh reverberating against my cheeks. It was nice just spinning with him under the sparkling lights.

Something soft planted itself in my chest, and I gently shooed it away. Jonas didn't need me mooning after him. Still, it slithered down, warming my chest right on the spot my heart tugged for the others. I settled for simply holding his hand, his warm one enveloping my own.

The song ended and we simply stood as the band picked up again, a fast tempo starting as dancers began to spin around our still forms again.

"Briar, I-" His gaze bounced between my eyes, something unspoken passing between us as he glanced down at my lips.

"Jonas…" I murmured, my voice almost lost in the roar of music. My mouth parted slightly as I leaned up on my toes, our mouths just scant inches from each other…

"Is that the fucking prince?"

I knew that voice, the same one that haunted my every waking moment, the one I knew as well as my own. With a gasp, I spun in Jonas' arms, locking eyes with the last person I imagined to be standing on a street in Eraston.

Cal.

CAL

Evin stood from behind his desk, motioning for us to follow. Avan's gaze flicked towards me, the simple sight of his face infuriating me. I hadn't always felt like this, no. His face used to incite passion, love, and, most of all, lust.

The way his face fell in sleep, his mask sliding away to reveal the man burdened with kingship; he was just Avan when we were together. No mask, no quips, no walls. I yearned for the Avan I knew before I was cast into the void by the council—a punishment for *his* crimes.

His lies have caught up to him, leaving us exactly where we were all those years ago, but now, we had more to lose than just each other.

Evin stopped at the door, whispering to the guard outside before motioning for us to follow. I stepped ahead of Avan, casting a furious glance his way, hoping to convey my extreme disappointment in one look. He huffed and rolled his eyes before following our small procession back into the atrium.

We passed marble column after marble column, moving into Cesa.

It was a bustling city, filled with more skin than I had seen in a long time. Witches passed quickly, long gossamer gowns flowing behind them, unbound hair cascading down their backs. Not so long ago, Avan and I had been part of this society, uncaring for human traditions of propriety. Ian had joined us not long after our dalliances in the library began, entering our small coven as if he'd been there forever.

Not every coven was intimate with each other, although it could be quite enjoyable, and Ian had his own affairs to deal with instead of inserting himself into our dynamic. Our magics complimented each other—my strong fire magic emboldening Avan and Ian's until we were the most powerful coven in centuries.

Then Avan had to go fuck it all up. For what? That damned crown? He didn't even want it.

Evin stopped us in front of a modest townhome, knocking twice on the wooden door. A small elf opened the door, their slight frame hidden behind the massive oak. A mop of curly hair covered their ears, flopping over their brow. Bright blue eyes peered at us suspiciously, as if they didn't often get visitors.

"Can I help you?" they asked, the deep timbre of their voice echoing out into the street.

"Is your patron at home?" Evin asked, peering over the top of the elf's head.

"Captain?" a soft voice wafted from inside the home. I knew that voice, and dread sliced through my chest. A woman appeared, draped in a silk dressing gown cinched at her waist. She started at the sight of us, her eyes flicking back and forth before all but dragging us through the door and into the foyer. "What the hell do you think you're doing, bringing them here? I'm on the council, Evin!" She waved the elf away, leaving our small party alone in the foyer.

Xinta whirled upon Avan and I, a finger pointed shakily at us. "What the fuck are you two doing out of the dungeons? Do war criminals get daily walks now, is that it? Are you bribing the good captain?" Her voice wavered from the anger roiling off her in waves.

"Xinta, they are here because I asked them to be." Evin soothed a hand down her back, immediately lowering her hackles. I rolled my eyes at the gesture, clicking my tongue against my teeth. "We need them," he spoke softly, afraid of possible listening ears.

"We most certainly do not. My shadows will do just fine on their own without these two bumbling idiots." She gestured to us, the glittering jewels adorning her hands flashing in the light.

"Their magic is more powerful than all of us combined, and what if we can find Briar? We can make some real changes with their help, and Delani will finally be stopped," Evin murmured to her, flicking his gaze to us before landing back on Xinta. "I need you to remove their bracelets. Please."

"I cannot, Evin. The council will have my head if they find out I was the one who removed them," Xinta protested.

"Then we'll make sure they never find out," Avan finally spoke up from where he'd been standing behind Evin. "You know what my magic can do. I can erase this whole encounter from your head so Orin will never know."

"Absolutely not. Neither you nor your magic will get anywhere near my memories. Like I said, we're doing fine on our own." Xinta crossed her arms, petulant as ever.

"Xinta…" Evin started.

"I call in my debt," I cut in, Xinta's gaze darting towards me. The color drained from her face, leaving an ashen mess in its wake. She shook her head, taking a small step back as if she could outrun a magically-binding contract. "You will remove the bracelets and allow Avan to erase the memories from your head—without any trickery from either party." I pointed the last part at Avan, his eyes rolling.

A deep orange magic burst from Xinta's body, wrapping around our bodies and lifting us from the floor. Long forgotten magic bound us together in a drunken bet from so many years ago, I forgot what it was even about. That night had ended with three less citadel guards and one life debt owed to me. Still, I never forgot it, waiting for the right time to call the debt in. There wasn't enough time to save Avan and I the first time, but I would use everything at my disposal to save Briar, even if it meant using the one ace I had up my sleeve. She is the very air that I breathe, and every day without her, I suffocated.

Xinta's head tilted back, magic flooding her features with a blinding light. Her mouth was open in a silent scream, and energy coursed through both our bodies in a pulsing tandem. The golden circles dropped from my wrists, clinking to the floor, followed by an echo from Avan's doing the same.

The orange magic whooshed back into Xinta, her body reabsorbing every last drop. When our bodies heaped onto the floor, I felt it: my own fiery magic flooding my veins. I felt positively giddy as my magic returned, that aching throb of Briar in my chest bringing me to tears. I gasped into my hands, burying my face into the warm callouses.

Avan gasped behind me, his evergreen magic weaving in and out of his fingers as he watched in amazement. He stopped as Xinta roused herself from the floor, glaring at me and then Avan.

"Well, get on with it. Fucking tricky witches. You all say Ian is bad, but you should take a look at the two of you." She waved her hand towards us, flopping back onto the wooden floor, resigned to her fate. Avan shot a string of magic towards Xinta, her eyes going glassy as he removed the memories of the past few minutes. Her eyes shuttered closed as Avan's magic lulled her into a deep sleep.

"Well, that went a little differently than I imagined." Evin crouched down to check Xinta's breathing, calling for her elf to whisk her away to her bedchambers. "You two certainly are surprising."

"Oh, you have no idea." Avan grinned, the glowing magic behind his eyes casting shadows across the floor.

The horse swayed me side to side, our small traveling group meandering down the dirt path. The tall peaks of the Erast mountain range were to the north of us, guiding our way. Our journey south from Cesa was uneventful, witches mostly carted along in opulent carriages paying no mind to the three cloaked travelers passing them by.

I had a hard time keeping my eyes open, dutifully ignoring Avan's persistent attempts at conversation. He refused to take the hint, trying to pull me into talk of the weather, how far we'd traveled, the shape of the mountains beside us.

"Avan, if you don't shut up, I'll shut you up myself," I snapped finally, silencing the incessant babble spouting from his mouth. He had a lot to make up for, and it wouldn't start with the travel to Eraston.

Ian's home city, nestled away in the mountains they were named for, was a gem hidden from the prying eyes of court. He'd made sure to erase most information about it when he came into his rank, citing the fact that the monarchy of old had all but wiped Belmare off the map in its quest for dominance. He wanted to protect what was precious to him, a sentiment I knew all too well.

That bloom within my chest was a warm reminder Briar was safe, hidden away with the rest of Ian's flock behind his impenetrable wards. I could feel her, the warm bubbling of her laugh, the way her nose scrunched up when she was deep in thought. It was a triumph that I didn't run my horse ragged to get to her.

Evin had been tight-lipped about the rest of his plans, stating that we needed to wait until we meet again with Briar and Ian. His broad back faced me in our procession, rigid and not a muscle out of place, ever the Captain of the Guard. I nudged my horse forward until I rode by Evin's side, companionable silence between us. It was a nice reprieve from Avan's pestering.

"Do you know how much longer it will be?" I asked.

He grunted, tilting his head side to side. "I would say by late evening, if we don't stop much. We will need to water the horses soon and get a bite to eat. Wouldn't want you two fainting off your horses." A sly grin worked up Evin's face, his teasing a balm to my frayed nerves.

"I'm made of sterner stuff. I was a guard, I'll have you know. I trained the same as you," I sniffed.

"Yes, but unlike me, you caught the attention of the pampered king." Evin nodded back towards Avan, the regality of his riding obvious even under the large cloak he wore. "Things tend to fall away when you live a lavish life."

He wasn't wrong. I relied on my magic more than a sword or dagger, horseback riding done more for fun more than necessity, and I couldn't remember the last time I'd donned the golden armor of the citadel.

"Love makes you do strange things," I replied, feeling a burn in my back that had little to do with my magic.

We stopped at a small river shortly after, the clear water beckoning us to its shores. The horses drank deeply while Avan and I stripped our shirts off and enjoyed the cool waters. It felt like ages since I'd enjoyed washing myself, our time spent in the castle and dungeons leaving a coat of grime that wasn't easily wiped away with a cloth. Avan stopped splashing the water on himself, staring at my form in silence. I could tell by the way his jaw worked that he had something to say, but I was content enjoying the way he worked the words in his mouth silently.

"I-I know I've wronged you, Calvin. I have a lot to atone for, both in the past and now, and I hope to show you the changes I can make." His hands rested in the moving water, gaze piercing me.

I let him stew for a few more minutes, rinsing the last of the dirt from my body and enjoying the way Avan's eyes followed the trail of water down my stomach. Atone, indeed. His mouth opened, and I could almost taste the words he wanted to say. Water splashed around my legs as I strode over to him, gripping his chin between my fingers. The bloom of desire in his eyes made me pause for just a moment, flashing memories of grasping hands and ripped clothing bubbling to the surface. I shoved them down, bringing his face closer to mine, letting the fire within me out to play.

"I've let you take charge and make some stupid decisions, Avan, and now it's not just affecting me and you. There are people to think about other than yourself. Your actions cause ripples that cast far out." I shoved his face away and left him to stew on that, splashing my way towards the shore, where Evin was struggling with a small fire.

I twisted my hand towards the sticks he had piled up, igniting them quickly. He peered up at me, not smiling, but his eyes less harsh as they flicked between me and Avan walking behind me.

"I didn't have a chance to grab much from the citadel, so you'll have to make do with river fish." Evin gestured towards the small pile beside him, freshly caught. He cleaned the fish quickly, stripping the scales and bones before piling the cast offs in a neat stack near the trees. He turned back around to our questioning gazes, his brow raised.

"What? It's for the rampkins." He shrugged as he walked back towards our small camp. "Cute little fuckers." The small, cat-like creatures hunted at night and were particularly fond of river fish.

"As long as they don't follow us. They're so creepy." Avan shuddered. Evin eyed him, scrunching his face up in the most show of emotion I'd seen on his face.

"They're adorable, claws and creepy eyes and all," Evin mumbled, stabbing each fish before roasting them over the fire.

We ate in silence, the crackling fire soothing the anger that had planted itself in my chest. I rubbed absentmindedly at the ache there; the closer we got to Briar, the more it bloomed into warmth rather than a stabbing icicle. Ian's wards prevented the full manifestation of our bond, but I could still feel her along the pulsing golden thread.

"So, it's true then? You are all bound together?" Evin nodded where my hand rubbed. "That hasn't been seen in many years." He munched on his fish thoughtfully.

"We aren't sure of the exact nature, but once Briar's magic matured, we found our way to each other, with a little help from Ian." I rolled my eyes at the easy explanation. Ian's meddling might have gotten us in this position in the first place, exposing Briar, but in the same token, it had brought her to us. It brought me back from the void, brought Avan and I...

Avan hummed, tilting his head back and forth. "She's a meta witch. Her powers stem from all there has been, what is, and what will be. Briar draws from the most primordial of our magic, connected to the very earth."

"She's an elemental witch? Like us?" Evin gestured between me and him. He drew his hand in a circle, an umber magic spreading from his palm to pull up small rocks and clumps of earth, twirling and moving them about in his hand, faster and faster until they were a blur.

"She is so much more than just an elemental witch, captain. Briar draws from the stores of the earth, her magic all encompassing. If she thinks it, she can do it—elemental, teleportation, binding, charms, wards, anything. She will be the most powerful of us all when she comes into her powers fully." Avan looked down at the half-eaten dinner in his hands, turning it over thoughtfully. How damning it must be to no longer be the most powerful witch. Shame.

Avan's lips twitched as he nodded towards Evin's hand, "You've been keeping secrets."

"It's more advantageous to keep the magic I have under wraps than flaunt it. Anyway, it's good to know about the little witchling. I hope, for her sake, that she chooses the correct side to play on," Evin said, rising before swishing his palm over the fire, damp earth from the river shores piling on top to extinguish it. "We must get going. If you're not going to finish that fish, leave it for the rampkins. They bring good luck for travelers."

Night came and we pushed on through the forests, Evin keeping a watchful eye on the dark trees surrounding us as well as the towering mountains on our side. We grew closer and closer to Eraston, the tug of Briar growing stronger and more powerful. I felt itchy under my skin, like buzzing bees had taken residence in my chest.

Avan sidled up next to me, grabbing my attention with a soft wave. "What will you say to her when we see her?"

"I'm sure we won't be doing a lot of talking." I grinned, warmth blooming in my stomach at the thought. Her sweet curves and plush lips haunted my every waking moment we were apart. I, after all, wasn't the one who lied to her. Avan would have to make his own amends.

"Quite presumptuous, aren't you, dear Calvin? What's to say she won't kick both of our asses to the curb? Aren't you afraid Briar won't want us there?" he questioned, his teasing tone cut with anxiety. I could see the hesitation in his gaze, looking to me for comfort.

I huffed a breath, looking at him fully. His brows were pulled low with a soft smile, those damn cheekbones easing some of my anger. Memories of nights long ago rushed to the surface, each licking kiss stoked by the fire of companionship we found in each other, his deft hands learning the planes of my body, my own learning the song of his. I cleared my throat, a blush I hoped he didn't see creeping up my neck.

"I imagine you can use your flowery words to woo her," I bit out, some of that anger returning.

"I don't want to trick her anymore, Cal. No more secrets, between any of us."

Oh.

Oh.

Well.

It wasn't enough to fully forgive him, and most of the forgiveness wasn't mine to give, but it tempered the flame rolling through me. I hummed in agreement, effectively ending the conversation as the forest broke around us, spitting us out onto a dirt road leading straight to Eraston.

At least, where Eraston should have been. Ian's wards were powerful, concealing the entire town he grew up in. The only sign of it was the faint shimmering of the wards against the night sky; no sounds, no lights, nothing to bely the living, breathing city beneath them.

Avan jumped from his horse, tying the mare to a low-hanging branch before approaching the wards. His hands hummed with magic, his eyes closing as he murmured soft words. Evin and I watched from afar, my knowledge of Avan's magic keeping me a good distance away. While he has vast amounts of control over his magic, I wouldn't put it past Ian to put in backdoor security if Avan were to try and break through—the only witch powerful enough to do so.

A soft tearing noise drew my attention towards Avan's hands, his magic not destroying the whole ward but simply creating a gate for us to travel through. Avan turned, grinning, not even a hair out of place for his efforts.

Soft noises wafted from the rip in Ian's wards, music wrapping around us in an invitation to enter. I stepped forward hesitantly, the tug in my chest urging me on as I moved past Evin and Avan into the soft glow of town lights.

I all but ran towards the town square, the nightly celebrations in full swing as I wove between couples, looking for the dark-haired beauty who encompassed my every thought. I cared not if Avan followed behind me, my sole focus finding Briar.

My head poked above the crowd, their twining bodies preventing me from moving at the pace I sought. Avan appeared behind me, Evin trailing behind with searching eyes. Avan's hand rose to mine, and I grasped it at the last second before nodding towards the town center.

There she was, twirling the night away in the arms of…

"Is that the fucking prince?"

BRIAR

A soft *oof* left his lips as I ran full force into Cal's waiting arms. His cinnamon scent enveloped me as I nestled deep into his arms.

"How?" my muffled voice asked.

"Well, it's a long story," he rumbled, bending until his cheek rested atop my head, placing a soft kiss in my hair. The absent tug of our bond flared to life at our connection, filling my chest with fire and spring.

I pulled back, finally noticing the other men standing behind him.

"Evin?" I raised a brow at Cal.

"Again. Long story." His cheeky grin did all sorts of things to my stomach, but there was another soft tug against the bond, drawing my eyes to the handsome figure behind the captain.

"Oh, Avan!" I pulled myself from Cal's arms and ran towards him. His face lit up as I approached, stopping just a foot away. "Hi," I whispered, suddenly shy. A thousand memories flashed behind my eyes–the way his face had fallen when he told Ameia and Delani about my powers, his laugh, the first time I saw him in the courtyard, his lies. My emotions were still tangled, but I was so happy to see him, my hands vibrated with the need to wrap my arms around him.

"Hello, sweet girl," he smiled softly at me. "How I've missed you." He took a tentative step forward, reaching his hand towards me before linking his fingers through mine.

"Avan. Calvin," Ian said, stepping to my side. I could feel the anger rolling off his body in waves. "You could have sent a message instead of slicing through my wards and leaving us vulnerable."

"You should know me better than that, my friend. I repaired them after we stepped through. I know how important keeping Eraston safe is to you," Avan said placatingly, taking a small step towards Ian. "It is good to see you, too. Thank you for keeping her safe. It seems we have things to discuss."

Avan's gaze darted behind Ian to where Jonas stepped up before gently pulling my body towards his. Where our sides touched, small sparks of magic burst across my skin. I sighed, leaning into him. Our small party was garnering attention from the surrounding townsfolk, people whispering behind their hands as they watched.

"We should go back to your townhome, Ian, and talk. Is that okay?" I peered up to him, his face unreadable before he nodded and turned away without a word.

Ainsley joined us with a huff, our baskets bouncing on her hips before she arched a brow at me and followed Ian. I reached behind me, fumbling with Cal's hand to pull him along with our little party, Jonas just a few steps behind.

I felt complete, all of them surrounding me. No matter the trials and tribulations I had to go through to get here, I knew that whatever happened, we would be okay.

"You three have a lot of explaining to do," Ian said, whirling upon our group once the door shut behind us. Ainsley planted a kiss on my cheek, murmuring that she would see me later, before all but running up the stairs. Her gaze caught mine at the top, a cheeky grin forming on her lips as she took off to her room.

"Well…" Cal started, rubbing his hand through his hair, odd red ends sticking up from his ministrations. "Evin here broke us out," he said cheekily.

I rolled my eyes, grinning despite myself. "I can see that. Thank you, Evin." I turned towards the stoic captain, giddiness rising in me at the faint blush that rose on his cheeks at my attention. He had been so kind to Jonas and me during my time in the citadel, and I wouldn't soon forget it. I wanted to peel away the stony facade of his personality, bit by bit, to reveal what was underneath.

"You're welcome, little one," Evin murmured.

"But, why? Aren't you in service to the crown?" Ian interjected.

Evin's dark hair was ruffled from days of travel, face bronzed from the sun, making his scar shine brightly. His lips pursed as his gaze flicked to me before settling back on Ian. "Queen Ameia, Delani, and the council have committed a great disservice to our country. The registrations system is so much more than tagging each witch who comes to Alehem – it takes a bit of their magic for the kingdom stores. That's how she's been able to stay in power for so long, and one of the reasons she kept Jonas locked away. He was privy to what was going on, and Delani whispered threats of regicide, an attempt to seize her powers."

"Right, and what are we to do about it?" Jonas snarked, gently nudging Avan from my side as he stepped forward to face Evin. "Ameia has amassed power greater than anything we've ever known…"

"Aside from her," Evin interjected, nodding towards me.

"What?" I whispered, my magic stirring to life inside of me at its mention. It purred like a content kitten, nestling within me and glowing with the ties of my bond.

"You. You are the first meta witch in eons, and your power only grows stronger each passing day." Evin crossed his arms, the gentle look in his eyes a sharp contrast to the huge form in front of me. "You are safe here, with Ian, but with Avan and Cal's magic, I felt you would be all but invisible from Ameia's prying eyes."

"What will you do now?" Cal asked.

"I'm sure the council has noticed our absence by now, and it's not safe for me to go back to Cesa. I will probably find work in Albone along the river." Evin's eyes darted away from mine, and something like anguish planted itself in my chest. I couldn't let him just walk away, not after everything he's done for me.

My gaze darted towards Ian, a silent plea passing between us. He rolled his eyes, nodding.

"You could stay here, with us," I said, taking a small step towards him. The delight that flared behind his mask ignited something within me, and I knew I made the right call. I linked my hand in his, tossing a soft smile his way.

"I'd like that, Briar," he murmured at me, heat passing between us, and something else threaded in my chest. It was something warm, not the fire of Cal's magic, but a crackling hearth, warm soup, a hug from someone you loved. Deep autumn bloomed along the bond, weaving in with my magic until it thrummed a golden hue.

I rubbed along my chest, Evin's eyes darting to the movement. He raised a brow in question, and I shook my head. There would be time to explore this later. I didn't even know if Evin possessed the magic to feel what was happening between us.

"So, we just stay here for the rest of our lives?" Avan's voice popped the small bubble Evin and I had found ourselves in, jarring my senses.

"You would burn the entire city to the ground from boredom, so no. You can't stay here forever," Ian drawled. "Plus, I'm sure Ainsley is itching to get back to Islar sooner rather than later. We can figure it out after that."

My eyes wandered up the stairs to where I'm sure my sister was listening around the corner. Now that I had all my men with me, I was certainly content to stay here forever, but Cal's wild nature and Avan's posturing would make for an interesting dynamic, coupled with Evin's stoic ease and Ian's powerful nature. And Jonas…

I looked at him, his gaze on me, something hidden in his eyes. Where did Jonas fit here, the wayward prince? I knew there was something timid between us, plus whatever unspoken bond he and Ian had. He fit here, too…somehow.

"I have, um, one more thing to show you before we retire for the night, little witchling. You should know everything before I stay here," Evin said, casting a look out the window at the streets. "Is there a back area to this place?" he asked Ian, who nodded and motioned for us to follow. I was intrigued – what could the mysterious captain of the citadel have to reveal to us?

The lights from the street didn't quite reach into the backyard of Ian's home, the mountains reaching towards the starry sky behind where Evin stood.

"You're going to love this, darling," Cal murmured in my ear.

"What's he going to do?" I whispered back.

"You'll see. Watch." He nudged my gaze back to Evin, who looked like he was holding his breath. He wove his hands in a complicated pattern before slamming them to the ground, a coppery magic flowing from his hands into the earth. A slab of granite emerged from the ground, flowing and moving with Evin's magic as his hands rose, weaving back and forth over the mineral. He stepped back, breathing heavily, before his gaze landed on me. Evin sketched a brow in my direction before flourishing his hands at the finished piece.

It was a stunning statue of a woman, her face tilted towards the sky as her hands reached in supplication. It was masterful, as if it had been carved by the capital's finest sculptor. I was stunned, the magnitude of Evin's magic leaving me speechless. He had magic, and what a beautiful thing it was.

"H-how did you hide this from the council?" Jonas choked out. Avan and Cal must have already known, their amused faces stuck on Jonas, Ian, and I as we took in this new information.

"It's easy to overlook those who mean nothing in the council's eyes," Evin stated simply. "My magic is simple, manipulating the earth below to create anything I wish. I could create housing, water systems, decimate cities, swallow armies whole. You get the idea as to why I'd want to hide this from the monarchy. They have enough earth elementals in their pockets; they didn't need another one." His eyes grew dark, shadows of the past roiling in the dark depths.

"This is amazing, Evin," I breathed, running my hand along the granite. Her supple curves were carved with a masterful hand, twisting and twining as if flesh instead of rock.

"Thank you, little one," Evin smiled softly. "I thought I should show you before you knew who you were accepting."

"You brought Avan and Cal back to me, and your kindness made all the difference in the trials. I knew who you were before your magic, Evin. Nothing's changed." I smiled at him, and his eyes grew from wary to hopeful.

"Can we talk?" My hands rubbed together nervously, Avan slowly lowering the teacup he'd been drinking from. We had gathered in the kitchen, Ian making a delicious smelling meal that made my mouth water, but this had to be taken care of.

"Of course, sweet girl," Avan said, shifting his eyes towards where Cal and Jonas sat before following me. Ian threw a soft smile my way before plating up Ainsley's plate. That eased some of the anxiety threading through my chest as I padded towards the parlor room.

Avan's nervous energy zoomed through our bond, zaps of electricity running through my body as we stared at each other in silence. I had a million questions running through my mind, and I tried to organize them in a cohesive train of thought.

"I'm sorry," Avan blurted. His face flooded with crimson as he took a step closer to me, entwining his hands with mine. Avan's apology took me by surprise; I was sure I would have to twist and wheedle it from him, but he was different now, wasn't he? Something fundamental had shifted within him.

I looked down at our hands, finding the courage to move my eyes to his. "You're right. You had no reason to hide this from me when a simple conversation would have sufficed. In a way, I'm glad you didn't, though. Otherwise, Jonas would still be rotting away in that prison cell and who knows where Ian would be. At least now, we can work together, and you can begin to fix the mistakes you've made." My lips twisted as I pulled my hand from his. "I'm not ready to forgive you. Trust is earned, not given because you made an apology. I understand, though. You have a lot to learn about talking to the people who love you, starting with Ian, Cal, and me. Not just talking – listening, too."

Avan chewed on that for a moment, working his jaw until he dropped his gaze from mine. "I did it to protect you."

"That doesn't excuse your actions, Avan," I said to him gently.

"I know. Your magic is so new, and it took me back to my days at the citadel, where I had no one to protect me. I couldn't help but to want to hide you away from the world's evil."

"If you hide a flower from the sun, it doesn't bloom. It simply wilts. That's what I felt like you were doing to me, wilting me in the dark. You didn't ask what I wanted; you simply took it without thinking of the consequences. I'm a person too, not just a summation of my magic. You have to let me flourish, beside me, not in front of me."

He nodded once before making to leave, but he stopped as our shoulders brushed against one another. He inhaled and closed his eyes, leaning into me before turning to walk away. My heart caught at the electricity that crackled between us, a quiet thump echoing in the small room. "I'll earn your forgiveness, even if I have to go to the ends of the earth. You're everything to me, and I'll prove it to you. I've made mistakes, but now, I'm going to make them right."

Avan's absence was a heavy weight inside me, and I ached at the sudden loneliness planted in my chest.

BRIAR

The next morning came and went, Ainsley chipper as always as she bounced around the house. Everyone loved her, their amused eyes watching as she wiped and tided Ian's already immaculate house. I knew she just needed something to do, and I hushed the men when they tried to take the cloth from her.

I found myself lazily stretched out on a couch, basking in the afternoon sun as Cal rubbed his hand up and down my arm. It was quiet, the only noises were our breathing and soft sounds from outside. I leaned my face up towards his, and he placed a small kiss on my nose.

"How did your talk go?" Cal murmured, snuggling down until his chin rested on top of my head.

I sighed, figuring the small conversation with Avan was probably easier to talk about. "It wasn't really a talk, so much as Avan attempting an apology and me setting him straight." My cheeks burned. "He said he was going to try and make things right." A sigh escaped my lips as I nuzzled into Cal's warm chest.

He hummed softly, vibrating my nose, before speaking, "Avan has fucked up, but is he different now? Something is different, and I can't put my finger on it. He doesn't seem as impulsive as he's been. You'd think one stint in a dungeon cell would temper that, but maybe the second one really stuck." I gasped, gently slapping his chest as we chuckled.

"How are you feeling about it?" Cal asked, suddenly somber again. I peered up at him, and his gaze searched mine.

Confused. Scared. Overwhelmed.

I tugged my lip between my teeth as I searched for the right words to sum up my emotions. There was this bubbling pit inside me, swirling with my magic until I felt like a buzzing cloud of zipping magic and uncomfortable emotions. I wasn't used to this, talking about how I was feeling with others. Being the older sister and sole provider for so many years placed a huge responsibility on my shoulders, and I couldn't afford to falter. It was like carrying around a giant rock on my shoulders as it slowly broke my back.

Cal's gaze softened and he reached between us to tug my lip free before placing a soft kiss on the bruised flesh. "You're safe with me, Briar. Your feelings are valid, and I'll never judge you for them."

Sighing, I chose to stare at the small circles I drew on Cal's chest with the pads of my fingers instead of into his piercing blue eyes. "I feel overwhelmed. So much has happened so quickly, and I feel like my life has been flipped on an axis. This bond has left me with so many questions, and I don't really know if what I'm feeling is because of that, or if it's truly me. I missed you and Avan so much, but I'm conflicted about the role he played in what happened with the council. Avan lied, hid so much from me, and I can't help but wonder if you knew anything about it." I buried my face into Cal's chest. "I'm scared. The crown knows about us, surely. Are we truly safe here in Eraston?"

"I had no part in Avan's deception," Cal growled, tensing beneath me. "Something broke in my heart the day the Queen took you. I couldn't reconcile the man I knew with the man lying to you and spelling out your very nature to the Queen. If she hadn't had a name to fear, would she still have taken those actions, or simply written you off as a wayward witch? We'll never know, and his inaction caused you harm. I don't know if I can forgive him for that." Cal's hands clenched against my back, shaking gently from the anger he held back.

Cal nuzzled his nose into my hair, his sharp exhale shifting dark curls over my face. "I-I have these feelings towards you, like my heart exists outside of my body. When you enter the room, my breath catches in my chest at your beauty. The thought that you considered even for a second that I would lie to you makes me want to tear this entire room apart. I would do that, you know, tear the world apart for you. When we were in the dungeons, all I could think about was your face, if you were safe. I don't know what I would do if I lost you."

My heart stuttered in my chest. The hopeless feeling I felt when Cal and Avan were imprisoned came back in full force, and I knew in my soul that I felt the same way. Avan had a lot of groveling to do, but I was here, with Cal, and I was going to enjoy every second.

I stretched to meet his lips in a slow, licking kiss, conveying my emotions into the simple physical touch. My fingers clung to his shirt, the fabric bunching in my palm like an anchor, weighing me down through the storm of emotions warring within me. Cal's mouth opened to mine, exploring and caressing every inch like he was memorizing it.

He pressed into me, rolling us on the couch until I was cushioned into the pillows underneath me. I groaned as he began undoing the buttons on my shirt, his strong hands slowly peeling away the fabric until I laid bare underneath him. Cal's hands roamed up the sensitive skin of my sides, his fingers gently brushing the underside of my breast and rising to tweak my aching nipples.

My hands curled into his hair as my hips rose of their own accord, grinding into the leg Cal had placed between mine. Zips of electricity shot through my body, our hips nudging together through the fabric separating us. We broke apart, Cal pressing into my chest gently with his hand as he kissed and licked down my stomach to place a kiss over my aching core.

"Stay still, darling. Wouldn't want the others to find us," Cal rumbled, his pupils blown wide as his gaze flicked up to catch mine. I nodded, watching as he bunched the fabric of my skirt in his hands and pushed it up to my hips. There was hunger in his gaze as he stared down at me, drinking in my form as he lowered himself, running his nose along the inner part of my thigh. He placed a kiss at the junction of my hips before his tongue licked languidly up my slit. I moaned softly, and he stopped, glaring up at me. "I thought I said to be quiet, darling. Do I have to make you?"

A thrill shot up my spine at the implication, Cal's strong hand grasping at my mouth to silence my cries. I moaned a little louder, testing him, and he rose to hover above me, his eyebrow cocking at my bratty threat.

"I see," is all he said. Cal reached down to my skirt, the soft fabric gripped in his hands. With a loud rip, he tore a strip from the hem of my skirt, yanking it down my legs, and tossed the rest of the ruined dress to the floor. Grinning, he leaned back over me and gently ran the fabric down the side of my cheek.

Cal raised his eyebrow as he held the torn cloth over my mouth—asking permission, to which I nodded enthusiastically—before gently tugging my lips open. He placed a kiss against my lips, our tongues warring for just a moment before Cal slipped the fabric into my mouth and tied it gently behind my head. It wasn't tight, by any means, and the cloth was too thin to really muffle any sound, but the heat throbbing in my core at the idea was heady.

"Good?" Cal asked.

I nodded, twisting my arms above my head and arching my back slowly. His gaze caught on the display of my breasts, taking his fill before he leaned back to resume his ministrations. Cal's nose nudged against my clit, his tongue spearing inside of me and curling ever so slightly to hit the spot that made me see stars. I gasped into the fabric, gripping onto the couch arm and arching my hips higher. I rode his face with reckless abandon, his licking and nudging coupled with the suggestive seduction of my bound mouth sending me flying over the edge as quickly as he'd started.

Cal grinned up at me as I laid there, boneless and gasping. My knuckles were white from how hard I was gripping the couch, and I whined a little behind the fabric as Cal pulled away from me. I darted my gaze towards the large bulge in his pants, and he teased me, slowly undoing his buttons and sliding his pants down his thighs. His cock sprang free, a small bead of wetness glistening at the tip, inviting me to lick and suck to my heart's desire. I looked up to him hopefully, arching and writhing against the cushions.

"Would you like a taste, darling? You've been such a good girl, I think you deserve to suck my cock, yes?" Oh, magic above, his filthy mouth would be my undoing. I nodded, and Cal moved to untie the cloth around my head. Cal sat back against the couch, his arms moving to rest against the back cushions. His legs spread invitingly, and my mouth watered as I nestled myself between his legs. Cal's cock jumped at me, and I took his stiff length in my hand, pumping up and down a few times and collecting the wetness at his tip to make the glide smoother.

Cal groaned, leaning his head back and closing his eyes as I moved my hand. I licked a long stripe up him, swirling my tongue around the head of his cock before taking him fully in my mouth. My hand gripped his base as I bobbed up and down, my tongue flattening before I rose with an audible pop. His soft moans spurred me on as I increased the pressure of my hand, magic gently slithering from my fingers to wrap around where my fingers grasped. The dark smoke swirled against him, creating a hazy cage that encased his sac and the base of his cock.

"What the…" Cal's head flew forward, his pupils blown to encompass everything but a small sliver of blue. His mouth dropped open, and his hands were gripping the couch cushions so hard, I feared they would rip. I stared up at him, licking long and slow up his cock as my magic pulsed gently against him in time with my heartbeats.

He moved suddenly with a snarl, hauling me up from the floor and spinning my body until my knees were spread against the cushions, my upper body draped over the back. With a swift crack, Cal's palm met my ass and I groaned into the couch. His hand soothed the burn before delivering another against the other side. He kissed down my back, gripping the flesh of my ass in his hands as his tongue speared inside me. He ate from me as if I were the last meal he'd ever have, licking and nipping against my flesh. A slow orgasm built, and just as I was ready to fly over the edge, Cal stood and thrust himself inside me in one movement.

The sudden fullness flung me over the precipice, and each thrust only heightened the sensations coursing through my body. Cal's hand wound through my waves, tugging my head back until my neck stretched deliciously, his cock angled just right as I rode through the aftershocks of my orgasm.

"Oh, Cal, pleaseee…" I whined, meeting each slap of his hips with a push of my own back against him. "Make me come again, please!" I was a sobbing mess, and Cal groaned as he pumped into me, grinding his hips once he was fully seated.

"Darling, you're going to have to beg harder than that," he grunted with gritted teeth.

I tugged at my magic, willing the cage around him to tighten as I turned to look at him with a grin. Cal's eyes rolled back as his pace picked up, his hands leaving indentations in my flesh. With each thrust of his hips, I pulled against my magic, gently tugging on Cal until his motions became frantic.

"You are a little minx," Cal groaned as I tugged just a little harder. His hand cracked against my ass again, making me release the magic with a huff. He blew against his fingers, and I could taste his cinnamon magic in the air. My stomach dropped as his hand reached in front of me, his fingers grazing my clit. His magic had warmed his fingers just slightly, the heat sending delicious sensations coursing through my body.

"I'm so close, darling. Come for me one more time, please." Cal nipped at my neck, his fingers circling against me, and each movement sent the two of us spiraling after one another, two suns colliding with each other, an explosion of heat and smoke. Cal grunted once, twice, before his hips ground against mine as he spent himself inside of me. He gasped, leaning over me and peppering soft kisses against my shoulder as he withdrew.

"That's my girl," he murmured against my skin. "Naughty thing." I could feel his smile, and I leaned back, searching for his lips. Cal met me with a languid kiss, his hands rubbing up and down my sides as he curled into me, slowly turning us until we were nestled against each other on the couch.

"I've missed you so much," I breathed, my eyes drooping as my body relaxed against him.

"I missed you too, darling, so fucking much," he murmured in response.

"Please tell me you two didn't just fuck on my receiving couch."

My eyes popped open as I sprang up, my gaze landing on Ian's amused face from where he stood in the doorway. He leaned his tall form against the frame, crossing his arms as he took in our naked bodies. There was an unmistakable heat there, his dark magic swirling in the depths of his emerald gaze.

"I wouldn't call it fucking, per say…" I trailed off.

"Oh, I would. You should see this thing she did with her magic, Ian. I came so hard, I thought I was going to pass out!" Cal draped his arm dramatically across his face, turning slightly to wink in my direction.

"You'll have to show me later, little bird. We have a problem." He tilted his head towards the stairs, to Ainsley's room. My heart dropped suddenly, and the warm feeling I'd had from the afternoon dissipated with his implication, my gaze bouncing between the two men. I sighed, grabbing my clothes and a blanket, holding them against myself as I moved to go to my rooms and change.

Ian stopped me with his hand, leaning down to give me a long kiss. His eyes held dark promises, his gaze lingering on the ripped fabric I held.

"Later," he whispered before tapping my ass and sending me on my way.

IAN

Briar's frown burned into my memories. Her sister had stopped prancing about my house, lost in thought before silent tears began rolling down her face. She took one look at me and bolted up the stairs. I knew she wanted to go home, and I thought to follow her to tell her she'd be able to go back soon, but the soft moans coming from my parlor waylaid my plans.

Briar wrapped a blanket around herself before making her way towards me, planting a soft kiss against my lips and wandering upstairs. Ainsley was up there; I'm sure she wanted to confide in her sister about, well, everything. They'd had so few moments together.

Cal raised his brow at me, lounging on the couch, bare as the day he was born. "What have you told her so far?"

I sighed, turmoil roiling in my chest. "I haven't told her anything."

"You probably should. She doesn't like secrets," he grunted, rising and making his way out of the lounge area. Cal stopped next to me, smelling of the sweet little thing who haunted my every thought, before slapping me on the shoulder and wandering to his rooms.

I did need to talk to Briar, but how could I bring it all up without influencing her towards my side? Eraston was one of many witch settlements outside the rule of the monarchy, built so long ago that the Queen has either forgotten or is content to let us continue our peaceful existence. Unfortunately, the way she's been taking magic from the realm is depleting our already low reserves of manna, the lifeforce of our magic.

Could Briar really turn the tides against her? How could I ask that of the little witch, to break her tenuous peace? I didn't know the answers to these questions, and her lingering taste in the room clouded my already murky thoughts.

I heard the soft murmurings of Briar and Ainsley above me, drawing my gaze towards the ceiling. I rest my hand on the railings, the pull of the strange bond in my chest willing me forward. The lingering feel of her magic trailed up the stairs, calling to me like a siren's song, and I couldn't help the way my hand pushed open the door to Ainsley's room. They sat on the bed together, their hands intertwined. Briar was freshly washed, her wet hair braided over her shoulder.

Ainsley turned away, quickly wiping the tears trailing down her cheeks. I could tell she wanted to go home, now that she'd assured herself her sister was okay. Ainsley had a life there, one she would throw to the winds if it kept Briar safe.

"Can we talk when you're done?" I shot towards Briar, angling my head at her room. She nodded, glancing at Ainsley before placing a kiss on her cheek and following me. I hated taking away time with her sister, but this was important.

"I'll be right back. We will figure this out, alright?" she whispered to

Ainsley before following me down the hall.

"What's up?" Briar asked, spinning to plop onto the bed. I couldn't help imagining her there, curled up between Jonas and myself, sleep still sinking its claws into her psyche. The way her body tucked into mine sent a shock of electricity right to my cock. I wanted to bury myself inside her, forget about all the bullshit outside this room, and just listen to her crying my name.

I shook my head, focusing on the problem at hand. There would be time later to bury my face between her legs.

"There are some things about Eraston and myself I thought would be important to tell you, before you hear them from someone else," I started, suddenly feeling very self-conscious. Avan, Cal, and Jonas were the only outsiders who knew about the spells I'd placed over the town to protect it. "I, um…"

Her hand snaked through mine, our fingers lacing together. The hopeful look she shot my way eased some of the fear planted in my chest. "I know how hard you work to make Eraston safe. Your secrets are safe with me."

I heaved a big breath in, sending a soft smile her way before continuing. "Eraston hasn't always been as plentiful as it is now. The monarchy had its thumb on the dark witches for a long time, our magic seen as something 'other' and treated as much. I saw my parents struggle for years under Ameia's rule, food taken from us to fuel the capital, our able-bodied workers sent to the fields and mines. I wanted better for us, so I worked my way through the ranks of the witch council, eventually becoming the ambassador of sorts for the dark witches."

Briar nodded once, squeezing my hand to let me know she was listening.

"I grew and learned more about my magic, utilizing Avan's teachings on warding to create the wards you've seen around the town. Little by little, Eraston was erased from the monarchy's watchful eye. I doubt Ameia fully forgot about us, but with my charm, I was able to direct her gaze elsewhere." I smile ruefully, memories flashing in my mind of all I'd done, the arms I had to twist on the council, the people I had to bribe. I'd do it all again to protect my people, to protect Briar. "When I formed the coven with Cal and Avan, it only strengthened the wards. When we broke apart, it was wholly on me to protect the wards."

"And now?" Briar asked.

I sighed. I didn't know what was going to happen with our coven; all I knew was she was at the center of our revolving magics somehow, tying us all together. "That's up to you, I think."

She mulled over my words as I anxiously awaited her answer. Would she also welcome Jonas, or even Evin, into the folds that had begun to tenuously weave themselves back together between us?

"I feel…like we were all meant to be together? You always talked about fate, and this seems to be the biggest thing fate has ever thrown my way, right? Jonas is…" Briar's breath caught, eyes sweeping to meet mine. "Jonas and I share something. I know you and he…"

I cut her off. "Briar, I *want* you to want Jonas, more than anything I've ever felt before. I know this feels right to me. Magic is more powerful in covens. Take a look at what Avan, Cal, and I shared. We may not have come together like Jonas and I did, but I love them like my own blood. With you and Jonas? And Evin?" I prompted as she blushed and nodded. "We would complete something I think has been forgotten for a very long time."

I pecked a kiss against her lips to seal my words, hopeful she would act on them. I loved Jonas, and my feelings for Briar only grew with each passing day. It would come together, somehow.

"We got off track," she giggled against my lips.

I sighed, pulling back and immediately missing the feel of her lips. "Ameia's power has become too corrupt. Her tradition of taking the magic of incoming witches to fuel her own is becoming a problem. She's taking more and more from each witch, leaving little power for the rest of us to draw from."

"Is that where I come in?" Briar asked softly, fear coating every word.

I nodded, my hand gripping hers like a lifeline. "I think your ability to control the very essence of magic would come in handy, but I can't ask that of you. Ameia and Delani have far-reaching power, vaster than just their magic. Their political hold over the kingdom isn't something that can simply be wiped out. It has to be systemic."

"Could it save Eraston? Jonas?" she said, hope leaking into her features. My heart warmed at the way her heart ached for Jonas, so similar to my own. I'd thought him lost so long ago; it wasn't even a possibility he could factor into my plans. He was here now, though, the crown prince in my townhome. I wanted to crow with joy at the thought of him safe, in my arms.

"Yes and save Jonas." I tweaked her nose. "If I didn't know any better, I'd say you have feelings for our crown prince."

The blush that encompassed her face was delicious, and the yearning from just a few moments ago blossomed in my chest again.

"Jonas deserves to live in peace," she said simply. "Without a sword hanging over his head."

"That he does, little bird. That he does," I sighed.

"Do you still love him?" she asked, suddenly finding the blanket underneath us extremely interesting.

I wrapped my fingers around her chin and pulled her gaze towards mine. "I love him with every fiber of my being, little bird. Just as much as I love you. Do you like him? It's alright if you do. I want nothing more than to wake up with both of you in my bed."

She nodded, gnawing on her lip in that insufferable way she does. I thumbed the bruised flesh out of her mouth and kissed the pain away.

"I'm fiercely protective of the things that matter most to me, little bird. You and Jonas are included in that. I see the way Jonas looks at you when he thinks no one is paying attention. He just needs time and space. He'll come around."

Briar leaned into me, and I wrapped my arms around her before leaning us back onto the bed. We laid in silence for a moment, my hand running absently through her waves. "What has your sister so upset?" I asked.

She sighed, a puff of air curling across my chest. "Ainsley is worried about Clarkston. She thinks the council will find him and something bad will happen. She wants to go back to Islar. I was trying to tell her what a horrible idea that was when you came in."

I hummed, turning over the idea in my mind. "There could be a way to both protect her and make her happy."

A soft purr interrupted me as Lucien joined us on the bed. He was an interesting cat–very untrusting at first, especially since his mistress was gone. He warmed up to me eventually, and as he curled up on my chest with a low rumble, I knew I had somehow been accepted by the little orange terror.

"With Avan here, placing a simple ward around Islar wouldn't be too out of the question," I continued. "It would avert the eyes of the council, not fully eclipse it like mine does for Eraston. Your sister and Clarkston could continue to live their lives without fear of consequence."

Briar sat up suddenly, her eyes glittering. "Truly?"

"Truly."

Her face broke into a wide grin as she tackled me back against the bed with a fierce kiss. Briar's hands roamed up to grab my face, tilting me back for her own perusal. Her long kisses reignited the fire her soft moans had stoked downstairs.

She pulled back all too soon, pecking a small kiss against my nose before lifting herself up. "I have to tell Ainsley. We can finish this later." She winked, making her way back to her sister.

I palmed my stiff length in my hand, groaning at the thought of her body above mine, the way her breasts swayed as she moved, her curls tossed haphazardly over her shoulder as her hands roamed my chest.

A soft cough drew my eyes open, landing on a pair of dark brown ones staring at me from the door. Jonas' heated gaze was focused solely on where my hand stroked myself, a muscle fluttering in his cheek as he turned to leave.

"Wait!" I called to him, jumping from the bed. My hand wove into his, stopping him from leaving. "Wait. I'm glad you're here. I've missed you." I raised my hand to touch his cheek, and the skin there pinked deliciously.

"I doubt that," Jonas gritted out, his gaze darting from mine. I stopped pulling against him, stepping back with a flurry of questions in my mind.

"What?"

"I just think if you had missed me so much, you would have rescued me from the dungeons years ago, instead of doing so because Briar asked you to." His words were like knives in my chest.

"Oh, Jonas, no." I pulled him towards me, his body stiff as I wrapped my arms around him. I leaned my cheek against his soft curls, the white hairs tickling against my lips as I murmured to him. "Your mother lied to us. She told the entire country you had been lost to the sands of Belmare. I thought you were dead," I choked, tears springing into my eyes.

His loss had shattered me, breaking me apart for years. I'd only just pieced myself back together when he reappeared. I had never felt love like I felt towards him, until Briar. The beam of light she shone onto my frayed soul was something I never thought I'd feel again.

"When I saw you in that cell, broken, something inside of me shattered. I wasn't going to leave you there, whether she asked me to or not. I wasn't going to lose you again," I murmured into his hair.

"I thought you left me there to rot, Ian. I never thought I would see the outside world again." His voice cracked, wetness from his tears soaking into my shirt. I hushed him, gently swiping my hand up and down his back in a soothing motion. I moved us to the bed, laying our bodies side by side.

"You're here now, Jonas, and I'll never let anything tear us apart again," I vowed, something sinking deep into my chest with the words. Our time apart was too vast, and so much had changed, but the way his eyes peered up at me was so familiar, so safe. I kissed his nose gently, pulling him into my chest with a crushing hug.

We laid like that for a while, slowly drifting off to sleep, any plans I had made flying out the window for the soft body in my arms.

Well, this was a problem.

Sometime in the night, Briar had found us curled together in bed and wiggled her way under the covers. We'd tossed and turned, nudging her between us so that her sleepy face was turned towards Jonas. Her ass? Perfectly arched into my cock.

I held back a groan as my hands roamed over her soft skin, hiking up the thin shirt she slept in. My mind couldn't help but preen at the way our bodies fit together so perfectly, Jonas on the other side sleeping just as soundly as she did.

Jonas and I had broken through the glass separating us last night, his fears laid naked before me. I would do whatever I needed to in order to gain back his trust, to ensure he never left my side again.

He was so different from when I last saw him, his mother weaving a web of lies that he'd been sent on a mission to Belmare, never to return. I'd mourned his loss, and the shock of him, skinny and dirty in that dungeon with Briar, was something I would have to work hard to overcome. I'd let him go, and now he was here again, whole and healthy. He was still Jonas underneath the trauma, his humor and bright eyes sparking through the darkness every so often, but the years alone under the citadel had hardened him. No longer was he the pampered prince looking for distraction in my arms. Jonas clung to Briar like a lifeline, their shared time sparking something heated between them.

Briar grunted in her sleep, wiggling against me as she got comfortable.

Her arms circled around Jonas, nudging against me as she moved him closer. She sighed and settled, curling her body between us. I looked down under the sheets, watching as my fist curled around her clothing, at the way the fabric slid up her creamy thigh.

Movement had my gaze snapping up, meeting Jonas' piercing eyes above Briar's head. He watched me with heat in his gaze, eyes flicking to where I'd just been entranced a moment ago. I raised a brow at him, not wanting to push him into something he wasn't comfortable with, but he grinned, lowering his mouth to press against Briar's forehead gently. If Jonas needed to forget everything in our bodies for a few moments, who was I to deny the prince?

Briar groaned, stretching in between us, reaching a sleepy hand up to thread into Jonas' curls. She tilted her face up towards him, eyes still shut as their lips met in a tender kiss. His mouth opened for hers, their tongues warring slowly with one another as magic crackled in the air. It was like each sip she took from one of us only amplified her powers.

Their eyes cracked open, bouncing between one another as Briar woke up fully. "Well, I wasn't expecting that as a wake up, but it was nice," she whispered. I nudged against her from behind, working my arm around to thumb at her nipple. Briar arched into my touch, tilting her head back until she found my heated gaze. "Good morning to you too, Ian." Her soft giggle sent a zip of electricity straight to my cock, and I buried my face into her hair with a groan.

Jonas captured her lips again, pulling her thigh across his hips as he plunged into her mouth. She moaned into him; our bodies were so close, I could feel the rumble of her voice in my chest. Something threaded between us, fiery heat and magic tying us all together. I could taste the icy winter of Jonas' water magic mingling with the star kissed night of Briar, and it was all I could do to hold myself back as they explored each other.

"C'mere," Briar said, breaking away and turning until it was Jonas and I staring into each other's eyes. "Kiss him, Ian. I want to taste the two of you."

My eyes searched Jonas', asking for permission to cross that tenuous line. He answered by leaning forward, taking my lips in his, and the sweet taste of him and Briar exploded along my tongue. Ours was a familiar dance, learned in the halls of the castle, his darkened room on starless nights, hands roaming each other's bodies until I knew his like my own. Memories flooded between us, so many lost years accumulating in one explosive kiss.

Jonas broke from me first, nipping at my bottom lip before turning to Briar. Her pupils were blown wide, watching us, squirming underneath where we met. She glanced towards me, reaching for my lips as she turned her body into me. Her lips took from mine hungrily, and Jonas snaked his hands around until one hand was plucking and pulling at the buttons of her shirt. His deft fingers found a pert rosy nipple to tease, and she groaned into my mouth. Jonas' other hand roamed over her hip, reaching between our bodies until his fingers trailed along my straining pants. I gasped into Briar's mouth, her stretching grin telling me she knew exactly what Jonas was doing.

"How do you want us, my star?" Jonas whispered in her ear. "Like this?" He rubbed against her ass, pushing her against me, both of us moaning at his movements.

Briar broke from me, gasping. Her gaze flicked between Jonas and me as she nibbled on her lip. She wanted to ask, I knew it as much as

I knew my own name, but would she utter those thoughts? Tell us her wishes? Would she be brave enough to ask, and would I be brave enough to answer?

"I want us all together, with you between Ian and me," she whispered, heat flaring across her cheeks. Brave girl.

IAN

I looked at Jonas, emotions warring across his face. Did he want that too? His gaze flicked to mine as he nodded. He rolled Briar underneath him and dove against her lips, crushing her to him. Jonas' hands made quick work of the rest of the buttons on her shirt until she laid bare beneath him, grasping at his clothes until his bare skin shone in the early morning sun. Jonas' form had filled out since he arrived at my home, his body healing along with his mind. It was a sight to behold, their bodies twining with each other as Jonas gently nudged his stiff length against Briar's soft body.

I moved myself behind Jonas, shooting Briar a wink over his shoulder as he mouthed down the column of her neck. My hands made quick work of his pants, his knees shuffling in the sheets as I worked them down his legs.

"You have too many clothes on, Ian," Briar whined, sitting herself and Jonas up to reach her hands towards me. I stilled her movements, placing kisses against her knuckles before sucking a soft digit into my mouth. Her lips opened with a pant, gaze focused solely on where her finger disappeared into my mouth.

"This is about all of us, and I'm going to make sure you both see stars. Don't worry about me, little bird. I'll have my fun, too." I shot her a wink before pushing her gently back onto the bed. Then, I pulled Jonas back to my chest, his whole body vibrating with need as I placed soft kisses against his jaw. My hands roamed over his body, skimming over his sides until they rested against his hips. "Would you like to see our little prince come undone, Briar?" I murmured.

She nodded, leaning back into the bed with her own hands sliding against her skin. Her eyes were caught on where my hands were squeezing Jonas' flesh, kneading his thighs as I worked my way up his legs. Jonas moaned as I took his cock in my hands, precum already beading at the tip in excitement. Briar watched as I worked him up and down, and Jonas threw his head back against my shoulder. Briar's fingers glided to her slit, working the digits in and out of her wetness with each pump I gave to Jonas. I would watch the two of them come apart underneath me and relish in the ecstasy on their faces.

Jonas' cock jumped in my hands, pulling my attention from Briar's brazenness and back to him. I leaned him over her, gently guiding him to nudge at her entrance. She was so wet, slicking over my fingers, and I worked two inside her along with the blunt head of Jonas' cock. She groaned, plucking at her nipples until she squirmed down onto us, her core sucking us into her body. Jonas nipped at her shoulder, stilling her movements until their gazes caught on one another. I moved my fingers as he pushed in with ease, their eyes locked on one another as their mouths fell open in twin movements.

He worked inside her slowly, taking all the time in the world. I watched his ass muscles flex with each inch until he was fully seated. She caught my gaze, smiling, before she pulled Jonas closer in a heated kiss. His ass was on perfect display for me, and I trailed my shining digits up his thigh to circle his tight muscles. I pushed one, then both, inside of him, the heat of his body wrapping around me until I couldn't imagine anywhere else I'd rather be.

My fingers worked him, moving opposite to his thrusts inside of Briar. I worked him open, scissoring my fingers until he writhed underneath me. I untied my pants, shoving them down my thighs until my cock sprang free. I pulled Jonas back from where he laid over Briar, putting my free fingers in his mouth to suck. His tongue laved over my fingers, and with a pop, I pulled them free to wrap around my cock. I moved his body down, gently pushing between his shoulders until his chest was flush with Briar's.

I tapped the head of my cock against his ass, teasing a few times until pushing in, inch by inch. My hips slammed against his as he pushed back, taking the full length of me in one movement.

"Finally," he breathed. "You're such a tease, Ian." He shot a wink over his shoulder. "And you still have too many clothes on." He eyed my shirt, half undone and draping across my chest. I pulled at the linen, tossing the offending garment across the room.

I grabbed Jonas' hips, learning his movements inside Briar as I fucked him into her. Our moans wove together in the sweetest symphony, sweat dripping down my brow as we came together. I leaned over Jonas, grabbing his chin and tilting it towards me as I took his lips in a bruising kiss. One hand snaked down his front, moving my fingers to frame Briar's pussy, spreading her apart while I plunged Jonas into her faster.

"Ah, fuck Ian, yesss," she hissed, grinding her hips up to meet my hand. I circled a finger over her swollen clit, tapping gently with each piston of Jonas' hips inside of her. Her body shuddered with a sudden orgasm, hands grasping at Jonas' ass, my hips, his hair. Briar's keening wail filled my senses, and I lost all semblance of control, my hips snapping into Jonas, bucking him into Briar as her wail turned into a soft scream. Magic crackled and wove between us, Briar's soft floral scent mingling with Jonas' harsh winter. My darkness trailed between them until the bond snapped tightly.

"Ian, I'm so fucking close. Please, let me come, please," Jonas babbled, leaning his head against Briar's chest before placing fervent kisses on her chest.

I moved my hand from Briar, circling around the base of Jonas' cock. "You'll come when I say you can. Our sweet little bird deserves to come again for her brilliant idea, hmm?" I hummed into Jonas' ear, his eyes rolling back as I gripped him. "Why don't you show Briar that talented mouth of yours?" Jonas nodded, and I pulled, dragging him back on the bed and out of Briar, until his mouth met her pussy.

She ground down into him as his tongue speared inside her, licking like it was his final meal. I continued fucking him, our hips slamming together and pushing his face further into Briar. Jonas groaned as I circled my hips, his licking and sucking growing quicker, and Briar's breathy gasps filling the room as she crested higher and higher. Jonas' cock jumped in my grip, aching for me to give him his release.

"Come, little bird. Sing that sweet siren song of yours for me," I grunted out. Her magic spooled from where her hands grasped the sheets, darkness leaking into the early morning sun until she exploded. I let go of Jonas at the same time, pumping him quickly until his release coated my fingers and he groaned into Briar's pussy.

"More, Ian, more!" Jonas whined, pushing back against my hips to encourage me. I gripped his hips in my hands, stroking myself inside him quickly until I roared with my own release.

My body flopped forward, enveloping Jonas in my arms as we laid together through the aftermath. Briar scooted down to us, her body shaking from exertion as Jonas bundled her in his arms as well.

"That was…" she started.

"Mind-blowing," I finished.

Jonas laughed, sending spasms down my already sensitive shaft, and I winced as I withdrew from him. Briar's magic swirled in the air, not fully engulfing the room but instead playing in the morning rays shining through the window. Jonas looked up at her tendrils, waving his hand to pull from the moisture in the air, creating small bubbles that floated with her magic. Briar watched with fascination, entwining her hands with Jonas' and kissing his palm.

"Your magic is stunning, Jonas," she murmured.

"I'll get full control back one day. Maybe I can even make it snow. I created an ice rink in the castle lobby one particularly hot summer day. Do you remember that?" He turned towards me.

"I remember falling on my ass and you laughing at me," I chuckled, the memory floating to the surface of my mind.

We all giggled and nestled into one another, content to lay together for the rest of the day. That couldn't happen of course, and after washing away our sweat and releases, we made our way downstairs to meet Evin and Ainsley in the kitchen. Ainsley's watery eyes turned towards me, and I remembered my promise to Briar last night.

"Where is Avan?" Briar asked, peering around the kitchen.

"I don't think he's up yet, little one," Evin responded, a whisk in his hands as he made lunch for us all. It smelled delicious, and while I was content making food for everyone, it was nice to have another competent cook in the kitchen.

She walked around the island to her sister, enveloping her in a tight hug. They murmured together, Briar wiping at Ainsley's tears as she explained our plan. Evin listened in, nodding and adding a few words here and there, and by the time he plated our food, Ainsley was smiling brightly.

Avan and Cal joined us a few moments later, rubbing their eyes as they fought the lingering kiss of sleep. Avan watched Briar through hooded eyes as she bounced around the kitchen. He needed a kick in the ass to stop pining after her. He'd apologized, but he hadn't shown anything worthwhile to prove to Briar that he's truly repentant.

"We need your help, Avan." Briar leaned her elbows against the counter towards Avan. Her hair spilled over her shoulder in a messy, wet braid, and her bright eyes landed on Avan's sleepy form. This was his opportunity to help, and I bit my tongue back from forcing him. If he was truly sorry, he wouldn't even blink at Briar's request.

"Help with what, sweet girl?" he asked around a mouthful of eggs. God, the man was repulsive sometimes.

"Ainsley wants to go back to Islar," Briar started. Avan started at that, his gaze darting between Ainsley and Briar's hopeful faces. I could see the emotions warring across his face, torn between wanting to protect them and appease them.

"Um…"

"Before you say no, Ian and I came up with a plan!" Briar interrupted. "With the two of you and your warding abilities, you can cast a protective ward around Islar."

"The amount of magic you're asking for is doable, but what about the maintenance? The wards around Eraston have to be redone every moon," Avan noted.

"They wouldn't be as intense as the Eraston wards. It would just be to avert the eyes of the capital. Anyone associated with them would be turned in another direction unless they knew what they were looking for. It could be refreshed less often and still hold the same protections," I offered, shooting a smile towards Briar. I was on her side here, and even if Avan refused, we would work something out.

He thought on that for a moment, a smile blooming on his face as he focused back on Briar. "That seems doable, sweet girl."

Ainsley squealed and clapped her hands as she jumped up and down. Her arms circled Avan in a tight squeeze before turning her attentions to her sister. Cal smiled at them as he grabbed the dishes from the counter.

It made my heart soar at the joy bubbling from Ainsley and Briar, and when they separated and Ainsley bounded up the stairs, Briar turned her attention to me and mouthed a silent thank you. Her eyes were fiery and alight with the adrenaline, and as her head cocked to the side, I followed her like the gone man I was.

She grabbed my shirt and slammed my back into the wall around the corner from the kitchen, snatching my lips in a bruising kiss.

"Thank you," she mumbled against me, working the buttons of my shirt between her fingers. "For this morning, for last night, for everything." Briar shoved the linen down my arms, turning her attention to my pants. I stilled her hands, chuckling at her ferocity.

"Little bird, they'll hear us in the kitchen."

The eyebrow Briar raised told me she really didn't give a shit, and if she didn't, neither did I. It *was* my house, after all.

CAL

My eyes wandered to where Ian and Briar had escaped, the telltale tendrils of her magic seeping into every crevice of the townhome. Every surface she touched held her mark, like her magic couldn't help but become imbued with everything she lingered upon.

I could feel the same magic within me, calling to me, ever since that fateful day in the meadow, where her big gray eyes had caught on mine. Evin had left for his room once breakfast was cleaned up, citing a much-needed bath, leaving Avan and me in the silence of the once-bustling kitchen.

Avan's gaze darted to mine every so often, his hands fiddling with the frayed edge of his shirt. Anger still simmered in my chest, and I had a hard time reconciling the man I knew with the man who had just proclaimed all those things to Briar.

"You, um, what are your plans for the day?" His attempt at small talk made me want to gouge my eyes out. We knew everything about each other; didn't he know how angry I was? How much I ached for him?

How much I wanted to scream at him, scream his name in ecstasy?

A crash sounded from the other room, and we both leapt from our skin at the noise. My feet carried me towards the door where Ian and Briar had just gone, but a thrum of desire down the bonds had Avan and I stopping in our tracks.

Briar's soft hum echoed down the hall, a dark moan right on its heels. My gaze darted towards Avan, his darkened eyes meeting mine in understanding. Briar and I had found our peace together, but I could tell by the tightening of Avan's jaw that they hadn't worked out that bump in their relationship quite yet.

A rhythmic thumping began just on the other side of the wall, and my heartbeat quickened in my chest with each soft moan that permeated the rock.

"Well, they're certainly quick about it," Avan sneered, but I could see through the haughty mask. He wanted nothing more than to be inside Briar, just like Ian was right at this very second.

"You're just jealous it isn't you in there right now," I shot back.

"And if I am?" He loomed over me, something stricken in his eyes. "If I wish I were the one making her moan, the one inside of her, making her eyes roll back? What if I am jealous, Calvin?" Avan carded his hands through his hair, making the strands stick out at odd angles. I loved seeing him like this, undone and without that damn mask. This was the true Avan, and I took sick pleasure at making him unravel.

I stepped closer, my chest brushing against his back as something stirred low within me, something I hadn't felt towards Avan in weeks. He needed to suffer, just a little bit, for all the damage he caused Briar. She deserved her happiness, and if that included Avan, that was fine, but he needed to crawl first.

"Do you remember the sounds she makes when you're inside her?" I asked callously, loving the way his pupils dilated at the memory. I ran my hands up and down his arms, eliciting a delicious shiver from both our bodies. Mine remembered his, every inch and plane, what made him buck in pleasure and groan with release, and I ached to relive those memories. I reached around his front, messing with the buttons of his pants until his hard length fell into my waiting palm. "The sounds she makes, so sweet," I murmured, nudging my nose along the column of his throat.

Avan hissed as I nipped his ear lobe, rocking his hips back into my quickly stiffening cock. "Ah, ah," I tsk at him, spinning him around to face me. Briar cried out at that moment, and Avan's gaze darted to the wall behind us. Her tinkling laugh was clear, and as I resumed my ministrations, his cock jumped in time with her breathy moans.

"Will you make it up to her, Avan? I burn for the taste of her on your tongue. Please? For me?" I gasped into his throat. I fumbled with my own pants, freeing my bobbing cock to work along with Avan's. Briar let out a soft moan as our cocks brushed against each other, Ian taking his sweet time indeed.

"I want to watch her come apart around you, hear those sweet moans as she takes both of us at the same time." My lips crashed against Avan's, our meeting harsh and vicious compared to the soft, plump lips of the woman just on the other side of the wall.

Briar's breathy moans filled my senses, the soft slap of flesh meaning Ian finally made good on his earlier promises. It was a beautiful melody, one I was all too familiar with by now, composed by the woman who had nestled her way into my heart.

I could almost see it, Ian's flexing muscles, Briars soft thighs clasped firmly against his hips, her feet nudging his ass to drive him deeper inside her. I pumped our cocks in my fist, the precum at the tips providing a smooth glide as we nudged ourselves against one another.

"Mmpf, you don't taste nearly as good as she does," I murmured, our noses brushing clumsily against each other as his head tilted to the side, his firm lips pressing against the column of my throat. I reached up, gripping his hair in my fist as I pulled his head back. He groaned heartily, his cock twitching in my grasp in time with Briar's sounds.

"You don't get to come until she does. You owe her at least that," I rumbled, locking my eyes with him. Avan's mouth was open in a soft 'o', gaze flicking from mine to where Briar was separated from us by a mere foot of stone.

"Please! Ian, pleeease!" Briar all but shouted. My eyes stayed glued to the stone wall as Briar's voice hitched higher and higher, Avan meeting me in a bruising kiss while our hips kicked against one another in a race to finish with her.

"Oh, fuck, Cal!" His breaths were a whisper in the room, the cool breeze of the open window carrying them like a secret out to the streets of Eraston. "Fuck, yes!"

All three of us came at once, sizzling magic zipping back and forth along our bond. The rumbles from Ian, Avan, and myself practically shook the entire house, earthy magic mingling with my fiery cinnamon and Briar's sweet darkness. There was a whisper of ice there, something new that hadn't been there before.

"You had better fucking make it right with her, Avan. For everything," I panted, my head tucked gently against his chest. We hadn't been together like this in so long, and shame burned through me as I looked at the sticky release coating our stomachs. It wasn't my place to fight the battles for Briar, and I felt sick at the satisfaction of making Avan come undone like that. "I don't give a fuck what she asks for, you give it to her."

His breaths came in heaving gasps as his forehead met my shoulder. "I will do anything for Briar. For you. Anything."

For some strange reason, I believed him.

The road from Eraston was a long one, Ian having made arrangements for his absence in the town. Ainsley insisted only Avan and Ian accompany them to Islar, but the growls and rumbles from the rest of us quickly squashed that plan.

"I risked everything to protect Briar. I'm not going to leave her defenseless on the road," Evin had argued, and I wasn't going to argue with him. With our combined magics, we encompassed most of the elemental powers in Alehem—we'd be able to protect Briar better than the entire citadel guard.

So, we packed and planned, and one early morning, we set out on a group of horses down the mountainous path. Ian wasn't confident the citadel wasn't watching his magical signature, and he didn't want to risk detection by hauling a group as large as ours halfway across the continent. The simple fact that he could even do it made my head spin. I was a powerful fire witch, but that was something entirely different.

We traveled well-worn roads, our forms hidden beneath voluminous cloaks, and I was thankful Eraston was so remote. It meant fewer people on the road who might recognize us.

Avan's horse sidled up next to mine, and he shot a cheeky grin my way. Heat bloomed in my chest, but I was still determined to make him repent for lying to Briar, so I rolled my eyes and clicked at my horse to bring me up to Evin.

We volleyed war stories back and forth, laughing at how similar our knight training was, despite the years that separated us. Evin, it turns out, was much younger than the rest of us—closer in age to Briar at the young age of thirty five.

"Thirty-five? That's it?" Briar asked, bringing her horse around his other side. Hers was a dappled mare, content to ride along gently underneath her mistress. I was sure Ian picked the most docile horse in all of Eraston for his little bird.

Evin laughed and nodded at her, his eyes alight. "I grew up in a small town south of Albone, in the forests between the river and the Eronmire sea. My parents lived their whole lives there, as had their parents before them. It was a logging town, but I had different aspirations. So, when the army recruiters showed up, I was eager to sign. I got this scar during training, you know?" He pointed to the long scar bisecting his face. "Another trainee was from Islar, and he hated that I had magic. He used an unspelled sword during practice one day. He ripped my face in half when I didn't block him quickly enough."

Briar paled, surely thinking of how quickly her own townspeople would have turned against her if Ian hadn't shown up when he did.

"What happened to him?" she whispered.

"Oh, nothing at first. We completed our training, and I bested him every chance I got. The higher ups liked me and when training finished, I was recruited to the citadel. You know the rest," Evin shrugged.

"Did you ever see him again?" I asked.

"No, but I heard he declined to continue his service and went back to his hometown. I do wonder what happened to him."

Military service was voluntary, but for those who came from poverty, it was the promise of a warm meal and bed that held them. If someone had money, or their parents did, they often enlisted for fame and glory. I can only imagine the disappointment the unknown man must have felt at the end of his training, especially coming from Islar, to have been bested by a witch.

Ainsley was up ahead, riding alongside Ian, her arms stretching high above her head as she twisted from side to side, stretching her body out. She turned to Briar, a pleading look on her face.

"Can we stop soon, please?" Ainsley dragged out the last word, her lip jutting out.

We'd been riding for quite some time, the sun rising through the sky as it reached its peak, and we hadn't stopped yet. I consulted Ian and Evin, their knowledge of the area greater than my own. A tavern was another hour or so away, and Evin said they served good ale.

The thatched roof appeared quickly, our group pushing their horses just a little faster than we'd been riding them in anticipation of a break and some food. It was a quiet inn, just the barmaid and a few patrons milling about the lower level. She eyed us as we entered, dismissing our cloaked party as we sat, clearly used to the unusual passing through in these parts.

Many rogue witches lived in the space between Sirith river and the Erast mountains, clanless and wandering the vast wilderness. Not many towns dotted the map, most congregating along the river or in the forests between them and the sea. It was easier to find supplies around the waterways, I assumed.

The food was placed unceremoniously on the table, the barmaid attempting to sneak glances under our hoods as she went. She swayed away from the table with our thanks as we dug in with gusto. We'd just eaten that morning and done nothing more than ride all day, but we ate like it had been days since our last meal.

My eyes wandered around the tavern, taking in the worn boards, the clean tables, the wary eyed patrons. What really caught my eye, though, was the large wanted poster, half hidden on the message board by the door. It had been to our backs as we walked in, or else I'm sure we would've turned right back around as soon as I caught Briar's bright eyes through the parchment.

"Shit," I cursed.

Everyone stared back at me, rendered drawings of the six of us with large, printed letters declaring our crimes, with a reward to boot. The council was really going all out for us. I nudged Evin, nodding towards the door and hoping he wouldn't draw too much attention to the poster.

His eyes widened under his hood and his whispered explanation to the rest of the group had us hurrying to finish and leave before the barmaid's flinty eyes put two and two together. Hopefully, she would be willing to forget our faces with the large tip we left amongst the empty dishes.

"What the fuck?" Avan rushed out as we sped away from the tavern.

"I know! Only a five thousand dilnar reward for each of us. I would think that would be at least doubled," Ian remarked, Briar rolling her eyes skyward.

Ainsley was quiet, her eyes darting to Briar every so often the further we traveled.

"We can turn back, you know. It's not that important for me to go back to Islar," I heard her say.

"Absolutely not, Ainsley Gresham," Briar replied, bristling. "A poster on the outskirts of the wastes isn't enough to derail the plan. It will work, this plan. I know it will, and you will be happy at home with Clarkston. We will visit often to replenish the wards, and everything will be fine." She nodded, as if her word was law.

Night fell, and our small group set up camp. We would probably reach Islar by tomorrow afternoon if we kept up our pace. I started the fire as Evin and Avan went to find something for us to eat. I could taste magic in the air, Avan weaving his to seek small game for Evin to hunt. They came back triumphant, exhilaration across both of their faces.

Ainsley passed out first, her head lolling against Briar's shoulder as her dinner slipped from her fingers. Briar bundled her sister up as Avan cast a ward around our encampment, enveloping us in a sheen of pearlescent magic. It shimmered as he worked, before turning translucent. His earthy magic crept through the air, and I could taste the familiarity on my tongue.

I'd been softening towards him, enough so that as he unrolled his blanket, I dragged mine towards his. I wasn't forgiving him, just using his body heat for the night. Right? Right.

Briar stood awkwardly at the other end of the fire, her eyes casting around, but always landing back on where Avan and I sat together. Ian murmured something in her ear before kissing her jaw and swatting her on the ass our way. He shook out his blanket and snuggled into Jonas' snoring form. She grinned as she walked up to us, her raised brow asking if she could join.

"C'mere, darling." I scooted back, leaving a warm spot for her between Avan and me. Having her between us was the most natural thing in the world, her ethereal beauty the perfect complement to whatever existed between myself and Avan. She was the final puzzle piece to our fractured coven, although I'm sure we would have a few tag-a-longs by the end of it, if the way Jonas and Evin looked after her was any indication.

Her warm body pressed back into mine, facing Avan as she snuggled in between us. His face turned nervous, glancing back at me before turning to Avan's back. Briar whined at the loss, reaching her hands towards him and turning him around to her.

"Cuddle with us, Avan. It's cold." I could almost hear her lip jut out, her big gray eyes going wide on him. It was irresistible, and I knew Avan would fall into her embrace easier than taking another breath.

"I don't want to crowd you, Briar," he mumbled, the blush on his cheeks faint from the dying fire. I shot another zip of magic towards the flames, encouraging them to grow and stay lit for the night. The last thing Briar needed was to lose the tip of her nose to the winter chill.

"It's not crowding if I ask you, silly." Her voice grew quiet, and her breaths evened out as she fell asleep. I could still see Avan's eyes glued to her, watching her drift away.

"You know, you've come a long way since you first met her," I murmured, content to let Briar sleep after the long day.

"Not far enough," he replied.

That was fair. Still, my heart had softened towards him. He truly was trying to make amends, and I couldn't keep beating him down if he was truly trying. He'd listened to Briar today, laughed with her, let her speak.

It was refreshing to watch him engage with someone and not try to be the one on top.

"Far enough to stop berating yourself," I said.

His eyes met mine over the tumble of Briar's hair, a million questions running through them. "What changed from this morning?"

I shrugged. "Watching you interact with her today, the easy way you said yes to helping her sister. The Avan I knew wouldn't have done so. You're trying."

He nodded wordlessly, gaze darting back to Briar's sleeping form.

"I fear it won't be enough," he whispered, almost to himself.

"Leave that decision to her, Avan, and get some sleep. She'll let you know when she's ready."

Avan stayed quiet, and my eyes drifted closed, but not before I heard a soft press of his lips against Briar's forehead.

BRIAR

Islar was the same as I remembered, quaint buildings peeking up over the hills we traveled, the shining river behind them. My heart ached a bit, but I knew we were here for good reason.

Ainsley brightened as soon as she saw the rooftops, and I giggled as she urged her horse forward just a bit faster. The buildings grew closer together the further we rode into town, and we left our horses tied in a public stable on the outskirts.

The sun was shining brightly, its warmth chasing away the winter chill in the air. I bundled my cloak tighter around my body, practically vibrating as Cal wrapped me in his arms.

"The townspeople might recognize us," I whispered, watching as the rest of the group tied neat knots in the horses' leads and unloaded their packs from the beasts' backs. "Avan!" I waved him over quickly. If anyone would know a disguising spell, it would be the trickster.

"Yes, sweetheart?" His eyes promised heat we couldn't fulfill, and a phantom finger trickled up my spine as I squirmed in Cal's arms until his wandering hands rubbed along my arms to still me.

"Quit that," I growled at Avan, his responding chuckle telling me he knew exactly what his eyes promised. "Do you know of a way to travel through town without recognition?"

Avan hummed, tilting his head side to side as he thought. Eventually, he shook his head, only to turn and whistle towards Ian, inclining his head toward our small group. "I don't, but Ian might. Tricky witch."

As Ian sidled up next to Avan, their warm bodies circling around me, and Avan's promises lacing through my entire body, lighting up the bonds between us. I couldn't help but groan softly at the thought of our bodies together like this, and as I did, each male gaze snapped to me, desire mirrored in their eyes.

Avan turned to explain my request to Ian, his eyes never leaving mine. Ian brightened, a salacious grin spreading across his lips as he grabbed my hands.

"You are a bright little thing, aren't you, Briar?" he murmured against my knuckles.

Magic above, they all needed to quit. I could only take so much.

Ian quickly explained the spell, weaving my hands with his as he showed me how to wave them over each person. I reached within myself, pulling and plucking at my magic until the starry shadows eclipsed each person, slightly morphing our features until we could blend in without drawing any attention.

Our steps were quick as we made our way down the streets, Ainsley a bit ahead of our group as she turned down each street with expert ease. She cut through a familiar courtyard, stopping in front of a darkened shopfront, cobwebs decorating the display window. My heart broke as I stopped next to her and peered into my dress shop. The forms were the same, the same draping silk I'd been working on when Ian worked his spell attached to a form near the back.

Ainsley's hand enveloped mine as Jonas laid his head against my shoulder. He was so in tune with whatever corded between us; he probably sensed the anxiety that ricocheted higher the longer we roamed through Islar. Jonas' curls tickled my cheek as he nuzzled into me, placing a soft kiss against my cheek before stepping back and allowing us to grieve.

"Are you going to open the shop back up?" I whispered to Ainsley.

"It won't be the same if you're not here," she replied. "Still, I think I could make it work. Plus, it will give me something to focus on while you're off adventuring." Ainsley's shoulder nudged into mine, and we shot quick smiles at each other before she pulled us across the courtyard.

My eyes scanned the street signs as Ainsley wove our group through Islar, landing on the one I knew she was looking for. Her hand pulled from mine as she all but sprinted towards Clarkston's house, scrambling up the steps to his home. Her knocks were quick and sharp, her feet shuffling anxiously as she waited for him to answer.

Clarkston's bright shock of hair was all I saw before Ainsley launched herself into his arms. As she pulled away, she remembered her hair was darker, eyes a different color, and she quickly explained to him who she was as we approached. I saw his eyes darken for a moment before his strong arms enveloped her small frame.

"Ains, oh gods, you're here." His voice cracked from emotion, and I didn't want to intrude on their sweet moment. Clarkston's eyes raised, taking in the rest of our group, lingering a bit on Evin's large form and

Ian's glowering face before snapping to me. "What the hell is going on?"

"Can we come in? It's quite the story," I chuckled. Clarkston stepped back, waving our group into his home. The door snapped behind us, Clarkston dragging Ainsley behind him roughly before depositing her into a chair in his parlor.

He rounded on us, eyes bright as he waved his hand for me to explain. I took a breath, shooting my magic out to remove the spell I'd put on all of us. As our normal faces emerged, Clarkston sucked in a gasp, his eyes growing wide.

"Wha-" He took a step back, throwing his arm across Ainsley in a vain attempt to protect her from the starry magic dissipating in the air. Clarkston's eyes narrowed and he took a step forward, but Evin slid in front of me, his arms crossing over his massive chest. Clarkston stopped, eyes growing wide as he took in my captain.

"If you'd let me explain?" I asked, poking my head around Evin's torso. Ainsley grabbed Clarkston's hand, shooting him a pleading look before dragging him to sit next to her.

"Briar can explain everything, Clark," she murmured to him.

"She has magic, Ains! What happened? Did they do something to her? To you?" He rounded on my sister, running his hands over her as she rolled her eyes.

"No, I'm fine. Briar is fine. Can she just explain, please? Will you listen, for me?" Ainsley pleaded to him, eyes growing wide.

No one could resist my sister's bright gaze like that, and Clarkston's features softened as he relaxed against her side. He nodded, gaze lingering on Evin as I stepped around him. Jonas, Cal, and Avan lounged against the wall, content to let me take the lead.

I explained everything, waving my hands as I talked. His eyes grew wider with each sentence, narrowing on Ian when I told him how he'd taken Ainsley to protect her, gasping when I told him about the trials. I ended on Evin, Avan, and Cal traveling from Cesa and how Ainsley had convinced us to bring her home.

"Briar says her magic can protect us, that we can live normal lives, Clark. Together." Ainsley's optimism in my magic was heartwarming, but Clarkston didn't look convinced. He remained silent, taking in all the information I'd just dumped on him while his hands gripped Ainsley's like a lifeline.

"I know it's a lot to take in, believe me," I laughed. "I only want to make sure Ainsley is happy and safe. I would never do anything to harm her."

"How do you know the army won't send someone here? This is your hometown, after all, and it's no secret you have a sister. Do you expect her to stay holed up in her home the entire time? What kind of life is that?" Clarkston spit out angrily. "How do you know the town won't find out there's an entire—a ward, you called it?—covering us? If they find out and trace it back to Ainsley, who knows what will happen? There's no magic in Islar, and we do a good job of keeping it that way."

"The spell is easier than most wards. It will simply deter anyone from looking for me or Ainsley. If someone from Cesa or Quantil comes looking, they will find themselves occupied with something else and miss the town entirely. Believe me when I say, Ainsley's safety is my top priority." I placed a hand over my heart, willing this stubborn man to listen to reason. If he loved my sister as much as he claimed, it would be an easy decision for him to accept my help.

Clarkston's eyes settled on Ainsley as he mulled over my offer.

His arms crossed protectively over his chest, and I could feel tension ratcheting up the longer he took. Finally, something clicked as he turned to my sister.

"I want you to move in with me, so I can keep an eye on you, Ains," Clarkston said, taking a step closer to Ainsley. He brought her hand to his lips, kissing each knuckle. "I promise to keep you safe, no matter what." Clarkston's gaze flicked to the rest of us, narrowing on where Evin and I stood.

"I know that, and I would love to live here, you know that." Ainsley brightened, a smile blooming on her face. She leapt into Clarkston's arms, burying her face into his shoulder, but the furious gaze he shot towards my group had my stomach churning in something other than gratitude.

My apartment looked the same, albeit much smaller with five towering bodies filling it. I missed Lucien's soft meow, the dark nights I spent reading in the window, his warm body my only companion. He was safe, back in Eraston with Merri looking in on him. Cats were funny like that, able to mostly take care of themselves.

"This is…cute," Jonas said, his lip curling slightly.

"It got the job done," I replied, placing my hands on my hips and shooting him a glare. "Plus, the shop is right down there, so it was a quick walk to work." I pointed out the window to my dark shop. A pang in my heart accompanied the motion; all my hard work would now be taken over by Ainsley.

"That Clarkston fellow was strange," Evin rumbled as he poked through my cabinets. I swatted at his arms before taking the cups he'd found, gathering us some water from the spout. He huffed, annoyed I took over from him, but softened as I shot a cheeky grin his way.

"He seems to be very protective of your sister," Ian added, his long form sprawled across my bed. He shifted with a wince, pulling a large down feather from the comforter before twisting it around his fingers and making it float.

"That's not a bad thing. He's going to be the one watching over her. I would rather he was overprotective than under," I rationalized, moving to snuggle against Ian on the bed. Evin hummed and came to stand over my bed. There was barely enough room for Ian and myself, and I poked my head up to look around at the rest of the men. "I should probably make the bed a bit bigger."

Ian grumbled, drawing me closer to him as I rolled away, giggling at his grasping hands. Magic sparked on my tongue as I shot the dark tendrils out, enlarging the bed until it was big enough for the six of us. It was comical how it filled the entire space now, the chair holding Avan smooshed against the window.

I flopped onto the bed, Avan still trying to extricate himself from the chair, and Cal reaching to curl me against his side. Ian floundered, looking between Jonas and me before I rolled my eyes and patted the bed.

That left Evin. Stoic, responsible Evin. I often saw the way his eyes tracked my form, dark with a repressed hunger that echoed my own. There was something there, dancing along the bond that we hadn't fully had the chance to explore yet.

"Well, that doesn't leave much room for walking around," I pondered. "Come sit, Evin." I nudged against his thigh with my toes, watching hunger bloom behind his eyes. There was something there, and I wanted nothing more than to dig into the dark crevasses of it and explore.

"You could have him too, you know." I started at the rugged voice in my head. It sounded suspiciously like a smug dark witch who was studiously avoiding my gaze.

"What if he doesn't want it?" I asked back in a small voice.

"He does, little bird. Look at the way he watches you. I think Evin would take you however he could have you, Briar."

Well. We would see about that. I shoved Ian from my side, raising my eyebrows towards Evin in a challenge. Whether he would take it or not…

Evin hesitated for the briefest of moments before he nodded and cozied up along my side. He was incredibly tense until my hand landed on his shoulder, scooting him down until our faces were just a few inches apart. "We should probably get some sleep," I offered to a chorus of begrudging grumbles. I knew my apartment wasn't ideal, but it was warm and dry. Soft puffs of breath began to fill the room as most of us drifted off to sleep until it was just Evin and me, faces carved in moonlight.

"Briar, I…" he started as his hand reached up towards my face. I leaned into his burning touch, something flickering to life deep inside my chest. Evin was so…cozy, like coming home, or a warm blanket. He was soft and protective, despite the harsh features he often wore. His sharp eyes looked at me now with something akin to reverence, and our noses brushed as he inched closer.

"Evin…"

A loud snort and slap against my bare thigh from Cal's hand jolted us from our haze. I grinned at Evin, a little annoyed our moment was broken but grateful for it, nonetheless.

"I bet Ainsley wouldn't mind if we bunked at her house," I said to him quietly.

"Please, for the love of magic, let's go," Jonas groaned from the edge of the bed. "If Ian moves one more inch, I'll be on the floor."

I huffed a laugh as we woke the rest up, my magic cracking through the air as I returned the bed to its normal size. I hesitated at the door, taking one last, forlorn look at my place of solitude. I wouldn't miss that part. I was so utterly grateful for the men who now surrounded me, but it was still sad to close this chapter. Ian placed a kiss against my cheek as he nudged me out the door, and I tasted ether in the air as his magic locked my home safely behind him.

Ainsley had a taste for the exquisite, her home one of the larger houses in Islar, filled to the brim with art and sculptures, a good meal always warming her kitchen. We had both been comfortable money-wise after our parents' deaths, and Ainsley was well off, thanks to my advice. She enjoyed the finer things in life, more so than I did. The house was empty, of course, but a quick shift of magic from Avan had the door swinging open to welcome us.

Evin's eyes widened as he stepped in, Avan and Cal wrestling around his large form, snarking at each other the entire time. I thought back to the night before, their warm bodies encompassing me, and heat rushed down the bond at my musings. Five pairs of eyes snapped to me, their dark gazes sending the heat straight to my core.

"I'm, uh, going to go wash up." I pointed a thumb at the ceiling, to the luxurious tub calling my name as I whirled quickly to ascend the stairs. I heard commotion behind me, men jostling amongst themselves as they followed me upstairs.

I giggled, sprinting through the hall and throwing my body into the bathroom, Cal and Avan hot on my heels. Avan's magic sprung to life, a shimmering ward appearing across the doorframe.

"You'll have to be quicker than that, boys," Avan grinned, flicking his fingers to close the door in Evin, Jonas, and Ian's growling faces.

"There might be food in the kitchen!" I shouted through the wood, hoping and praying Ainsley hadn't canceled her food delivery service before she left. I spun around to Cal and Avan's feral grins. "I was serious about washing up." I shook my finger at them.

"And I'm serious about seeing your soapy ass riding my cock, darling. Start the water." Cal prowled towards me, gripping my chin between his fingers and nipping at my lips. I flicked my magic out to the tap, steam rising from the pouring water. I heard fabric ripping, and my heaving chest was exposed to the air as Cal tore my dirty dress from my body. "So perfect," he murmured, palming my breasts in his calloused hands.

Avan shuffled around in the potions lining the walls, tipping a crystal soap bottle into the bath. His gaze landed on me, heating as he took in my naked form. Deft fingers quickly divested him of his clothing, his cock bobbing in the air as he made his way to my back. I fumbled with Cal's shirt, rucking the fabric up over his head as Avan planted kisses along my bare shoulders. His cock nudged against my ass, making promises I sorely wanted him to keep.

Cal sprang forward into my palm, and I hungrily moved my hand up and down his thick shaft, my lips searching for his as Avan pushed our bodies towards the large tub. I hissed as I sank into the water, Cal and Avan's roaming hands soaping up my skin and washing away the dirt from the past few days.

I moaned, leaning back into Avan as his hands wrapped around my front, soaping up and down my chest. His fingers stopped to pluck a sensuous melody against my nipples, and my groan echoed around the tiled room.

"I want both of you, please, right now," I pleaded, and Cal's gaze flicked over my shoulder, heating as he caught Avan's eyes. Understanding passed between the two of them, and my heart ached at the reconciliation I found in Cal's eyes. Things were healing between us, Avan changing so much, proving he really wanted to work on himself. It was a lot to ask of him, the stubborn man, but it seemed like a weight had lifted from his shoulders and I got to peek at the person underneath the mask.

"I'll give you the world on a platter, love. Anything you ask, it's yours," Avan mumbled into my shoulder, his hand drifting under the water to plunge two fingers into my needy core. Cal watched with heated eyes as the water sloshed around us, Avan's movements throwing me into a wailing frenzy.

Cal shuffled forward, palming his length and nudging it against Avan's fingers. He slid in gently, Avan moving his fingers to pump in and out opposite of Cal's cock. I saw stars, my magic spooling from my fingertips to wrap around us. I was losing control of the leash I had over it, and the tendrils wrapped lovingly through Avan and Cal's hair like a caress.

The full feeling of both of them inside me was heady, and I rocked forward onto Cal, spreading my fingers across the auburn curls on his chest.

"Do you like both of us in you, darling? Do you want Avan to fill you with his cock?" Cal whispered, as if the idea was just this side of naughty.

"Oh, fuck yes," I moaned, swirling my hips against Cal. Avan chuckled behind me darkly and withdrew his fingers, reaching over my shoulder and popping them into Cal's mouth.

"Doesn't she taste amazing, Cal?" Avan asked as he notched himself against my opening. I rocked back against the blunt head of his cock, urging him inside. Cal licked up the column of my throat, humming in response.

The pressure from Avan nudging against my opening was overwhelming, but I gasped as he popped inside along Cal, the duality of their thrusts sending zapping sensations up and down my body. I shivered, stilling my body as they began working themselves in and out of my channel in a slow rhythm. Each drag and pull of their cocks inside me had my breath hitching higher and higher, and when Cal worked his hand between us to pluck at my clit, I exploded.

"Cal!" my moan echoed across the tile. "Avan!" I shouted.

Ether coated the air as my magic erupted around us, sending droplets of water cascading in a rainfall around the bathroom, and I cried out, my core spasming around Cal and Avan. They grunted, spools of magic twirling and weaving with mine, adding to the effect. Plants sprang to life through the tiles as sparks of fire trailed along my starry magic. I leaned forward, huffing against Cal's chest as Avan withdrew from me, their hands rubbing against my skin as Cal nudged me through the aftershocks.

He pulled out sharply as I caught my breath, and Avan replaced him quickly, thrusting a few times before removing himself. Back and forth they went, dragging me higher and higher with them. I wasn't sure if my body or magic could handle another explosive orgasm, but I was determined to see it through.

"That's it, darling. Show Avan how well you come for us; show us what our cocks do to you, how wet we make you." Cal replaced Avan just as I crested over the edge.

"Oh, fuck!" I gasped out, my orgasm surging through me. Cal was inside me, his thrusts growing erratic as he chased me to the finish. He groaned, biting into my shoulder as he came. I turned to Avan, chest heaving as the water barely sloshed around our bare bodies from the explosion of my magic, and I bent forward taking his stiff length into my mouth.

He gasped down at me, threading his fingers gently into my wet curls. Avan's eyes bloomed with gold-rimmed darkness, his gaze focused on where I took him into my mouth. I licked up his length, swirling my tongue around the head before I took him into my mouth fully. I tasted the tangy sweetness of my own release on him, cut with the soapy freshness of the bath. I hummed along his length as my hand fisted around his base.

"Shit, love, you're going to make me come undone," Avan ground out. "Anything, anything you ask, it's yours, please!" he shouted as I flattened my tongue against him, power thrumming through his fingertips. I cradled his sac in my hands, gently kneading, and with a twist and suck of my mouth, he cried out, release spilling down my throat.

I drank every drop eagerly, grinning up at Avan as I licked my swollen lips. I tweaked his nose before sitting up, fully taking in the havoc we wreaked on Ainsley's bathroom. My fingers trailed across the leafy vines surrounding the tub, the thrum of magic still zapping through them.

"Oops," I giggled, waving my hands until the magic disappeared, plants sucking back within themselves and cracked tiles snapping back together. "I should probably get a better hold on my magic so that this doesn't happen again."

"Or…we just keep practicing?" Cal pulled me back against him, his already-hard length pushing into my back while Avan dived down, licking along my seam with a groan.

Practice, indeed.

EVIN

I could hear her sweet cries echoing through the house, my straining length pushing into the ties of my pants. I'd wanted her for so long, but I could be a patient man. I'd take my time with the sweet little witchling. She deserved that much.

"You're going to burn a hole through the ceiling," Ian drawled, his long limbs sprawled across the couch. He had procured an apple from somewhere in the kitchen, tossing it up and down, hovering it every so often with that dark, swirling magic of his.

My gaze darted again as the ceiling thumped, followed by a huge shudder through the house. Briar's magic coated every surface, and she was taking full advantage of Jonas' attentions at the moment. Her power continued to grow, and I could feel it coating my tongue. She was powerful before, but the more she interacted with each powerful witch of her coven, it only grew.

I wondered how our magic would intertwine, my grounding earth powers weaving into her starry smoke. It seemed like her magic was binding in a way, bringing together the different branches of magic within our country and making them stronger.

Cal's fire magic came easier to him, and I had seen Jonas using his water magic to extinguish more than one fire. We'd been here a week or so, Ainsley settling into her new life with Clarkston, Briar's gentle hand guiding her through the dress shop's daily routines.

Clarkston was…interesting. He was stoic, but always offering a smile to Ainsley. He regarded the rest of us—especially me—with distaste at best. I often caught an angry glare sent my way when no one else was looking. I dismissed the man, his controlling nature a product of Ian taking his love. I sighed, a thump and giggle sounding from above.

Meanwhile, the rest of us were growing restless. Ian prowled through the house, snarking at the drop of a hat. The only time he wasn't crabby was when he was buried inside Briar or Jonas. Cal and Avan fought as they had been, but they would often sneak off together or grab Briar's hands and whisk her away upstairs.

Then, there was me. I felt useless, without a purpose, my hands itching to help however I could. I was used to controlling the patrols of an entire citadel, working with recruits, checking on inventories, answering questions. Now? Nothing. I didn't feel settled in my new spot within Briar's coven, so I did the only thing I knew how to do.

Work.

She found me one morning out behind her sister's home, elbows deep in the damp, dark earth. I'd found a particularly sad-looking lilac bush and was intent on transplanting it to a sunnier spot when I heard her voice calling to me.

I sat back on my heels, my eyesight blurry in the bright afternoon sun, when I caught her figure coming from the house towards me. My heart galloped in my chest at the sight. Her rich, dark hair was piled onto her head, soft tendrils framing her face and swaying in the slight breeze. She wore a plain dress with a knitted sweater overtop to ward away the chill in the air, and she held a dripping glass of water in her small hands. She looked absolutely stunning.

"Briar!" I called to her, waving my hand so she could see where I knelt in the dirt. We'd been skating around each other this whole time, and my hands itched to take her face in my hands as she smiled down at me.

"I've been looking for you," she said, kneeling down into the dirt with me. "What are you doing?"

I explained everything to her, wiping the dirt from my hands and reaching for the glass of water she extended my way. I drank it gratefully. While winter was coming, it was still hot enough outside that I sweat as I worked the bush from the ground.

"Why don't you just use your magic?" Briar asked, tilting her head to the side.

I chuckled. "Magic might not always be there. It isn't good to rely on it like a limb. Think of it more as a tool for you to use. Plus, it's way more satisfying to pull roots from the earth with my bare hands." I shot a wink towards her, and a delicious bloom of red spread across her cheeks.

"Magic can be useful, of course," I continued, digging more of the dirt away with my hands. "But nothing beats getting yourself a little dirty from time to time." She giggled, and I straightened, blushing hard as I focused on the implication of my words.

"Dirty minded little minx."

"I know what you meant, Evin. It's okay," she said between laughs.

I smiled at her, and we sat in companionable silence for a moment until I was ready to pull the bush from the dirt. I motioned her back a few steps—nothing hurts worse than a wayward branch against the skin—and yanked at the base until it freed itself from the ground.

I carried it to the other side of the yard, placing it in the already-dug hole and patting loose dirt around it. I straightened, shooting a smile back towards her, but it faltered at the sight of her face. Her lips were parted slightly, small pants coming from her mouth as her eyes zeroed in on the bulging muscles of my arms. I curled my fingers in on themselves, and the flex of the muscles made Briar snap her gaze to mine.

"I'm sorry, I didn't mean to stare." Her voice carried across the small expanse of lawn between us, and all I wanted to do was eat up that space and wrap her in my arms.

"It's alright, little witchling," I said instead, letting a little bit of the heat I felt in my gut show through my eyes. Maybe she would take me up those stairs behind her and our magic could finally collide. I wouldn't mind a bit.

"I like that," she breathed, taking a step closer to me.

"What?" I questioned, my body tense as she sidled up to me, her hands reaching tentatively for my body.

"When you call me little witchling." She ran her hand down my sweaty chest, curling her fingers in the springy curls. "I like the way you look at me, the way you protect me, even if I don't need it."

I chuckled darkly, thinking of her fiddling with the fire last night. Cal was already asleep, and her soft skin didn't need to get burned on the logs when I was right there.

"It's my job to protect those I care about," I said. "No thanks are needed."

Her gray eyes peered up at me, framed by thick dark lashes and filled with desire. I curled down to her, my forehead meeting hers as our eyes searched each other's. She reached up on her toes, her mouth just a hairs breadth away from mine, our breaths mingling together. She tasted like earl gray tea and honey, and as her hair skimmed my cheeks, I caught the scent of lilies. Briar was irresistible, and I couldn't really blame anyone other than myself when I closed the gap between us.

Briar's lips molded to mine like she was made for me, her arms wrapping around my middle as I caught her cheek between my palms. She was so tiny, my body engulfed hers as we stepped closer to one another.

I groaned into her as she nipped at my lips, begging for entry. I wanted to take my time with her, show her exactly how reverently I wanted to explore her body, but as her tongue plunged into my mouth, I couldn't hold back anymore. A growl ripped from my throat as I hitched her legs up around my waist and stomped towards the house.

We ignored the whoops and cheers from the peanut gallery in the living room as I raced our bodies up the stairs to the room Briar had claimed for herself. I set her against the edge of the bed, rucking the skirt of her dress up around her waist, peppering kisses along her leg.

Briar's hands twisted in my hair, nudging her hips into the air to meet my mouth as I worked her leg up higher and higher. This wasn't going to be soft and slow; I could feel my erection straining against my pants at how hard I ached to bury myself to the hilt inside of her.

"Evin, you don't know how long I've waited for this," Briar panted, her noises turning into a moan as I reached her swollen pussy and speared my tongue inside. She tasted as good as she looked, salty and sweet all at once. I ate her like a dying man, flicking my tongue inside of her as I nuzzled my nose against her clit. She fluttered around me, the stirrings of an orgasm already beginning. Did the others deny her this? Had she ever been brought to and from the brink of ecstasy? I would show her that the anticipation is even more sweet than the finale.

I slowed my licks, her gaze snapping to me. I sat back, bringing my hand up, and thrust two fingers inside of her. Briar's head dropped back with a long moan, my fingers dragging along inside of her agonizingly slow. She nudged her hips into my hand, and each time she began to flutter around my fingers I drew back, pumping into her shallowly.

"Ah, ah, little witchling. You have much to learn," I admonished, rising above her to mouth along her fabric-covered breasts. I swirled my tongue around each nipple, not quite touching her aching tips but providing enough stimulation from the wool to keep her simmering.

"I don't want to learn, Evin, I want you to fuck me. Please," she added as an afterthought.

"You are careless with your magic. It spins and swirls around this house every time you come. Can you hold onto the magic for me? I can make it worth your while." My lips caressed her skin with each word, goosebumps snaking up her arms. I kept my fingers inside of her, slowing the pace until she looked at me. "You need to learn control."

Briar groaned, flopping back fully onto the bed and whining, swaying her hips to try and find friction on my fingers. "I don't want to learn control right now, please! I've waited so long for you, *please*."

"That might work on the others, little witchling, but I know you can control yourself." I withdrew my fingers at her groan, popping them into my mouth and rolling my eyes back at the taste. "Sweet. Would you like a taste?" I leaned over her, cocking a brow.

She nodded and I opened my mouth, letting a thin string of spit fall from my lips past her waiting lips. I dove down quickly, swiping my tongue into her mouth and pressing my erection into the skirts ruffled around her hips. I knew she could feel me through the fabric but denying her was the sweetest pleasure.

Briar's legs wrapped around my hips, and despite my best efforts to pin her down, she flipped our bodies until I laid back against the bed, her hips straddling mine. She gathered her skirts in her hands and moved back and forth against my straining cock, the lips of her pussy spread as she sought the friction I'd withheld from her.

I groaned, my hands gripping her hips to slow her movements. "Gentle now, witchling, gentle." She let her skirts fall, fumbling with the ties at my pants and working them down my legs. My cock bobbed forward, and her eyes grew wide as she took me in.

"Oh, yes, that will do nicely." Briar's hands wrapped around my girth, her mouth soon following as she swallowed me until her lips met her hands. I twisted my fingers in her hair, gently tugging as she bobbed up and down my shaft, groaning when her hands began twisting in tandem.

"Fuck, Briar, you're going to make me come if you keep doing that," I gritted out, gently pulling at her hair until she was licking and sucking against my tip. I collared her throat, pushing her back until her eyes met mine before stealing a kiss from her lips.

"Control, witchling. Remember?" I panted against her mouth, trying to remind myself more than her. She nodded, rising to her full height as my hands fell to the side. I leaned back on my elbows, ready to enjoy the full view of her nakedness.

Briar's hands pulled at her clothes, swiping the sweater from over her head and plucking at the buttons along her dress until it fell away with a flutter. She was glorious, wide hips and teardrop shaped breasts, small constellations of freckles dotting her stomach. I leaned up and gathered her against me, placing small kisses on each dark spot. I stood, bringing her with me as I turned her back over onto the mattress, mouthing kisses along her skin.

She grasped my cock in her hands, guiding me to her entrance as I pushed inside slowly. Briar's mouth popped open into an 'o', the stretch of her wrapping around me like a velvet heat. I stilled as our hips bumped against each other, catching her lips in mine as I began a slow rhythm. Briar swirled her hips to meet each of my thrusts, the fluttering around me growing more fervent with each pass. I slowed myself, gritting my teeth, Briar's frustrated growl echoing through the room.

"Moreeee!" she cried, grasping at my hips as I pulled from her.

"Control. Do you feel your magic?" I asked, palming my length and rubbing it up and down her slit. She nodded, panting. I could taste the stirrings of magic in the room, but nothing like when she was with the others. "Keep it inside, and I'll let you come. I promise."

We went like that for a few more moments, my barely-controlled thrusts growing more erratic, her eyes wild and focused on where I entered her.

"I have it, Evin. Please, let me come," Briar babbled as I withdrew once more, hanging on by a mere thread as the tip of my cock barely nudged inside her. Losing my last bit of control, I thrust fully inside, setting a bruising pace as I hitched her legs up to fold against her chest. My hands gripped at her hips, tilting her slightly up and hitting that tender spot inside her that I'd been neglecting.

She shattered around me but kept a tight leash on her explosive magic as stars whirled inside of her eyes. I lost it fully, slamming into her wet pussy, her release coating my cock and creating a delicious glide as I slid in and out of her.

"Fuuuu—" I groaned, slamming home one last time and spilling inside of her. The aftershocks of her orgasm fluttered around my sensitive cock, drawing out more pleasure than I'd experienced…well…ever. It was like seeing a god, brightness exploding behind my eyes as I came.

I panted above her, Briar's hands sliding up and down my back as I released her legs from between us. "Fuck, little one, that was intense," I gasped out.

She chuckled and brought her hand between our faces. The dark brown of my magic mingled with her starry darkness as she wove the tendrils between each finger before sucking it back into her hand.

"I don't know, I could probably use a little more practice." She grinned at me.

I chuckled, flipping our bodies until she hovered over me, my hands dragging her hips until her perfect pussy was above my mouth.

"Then let's practice."

Briar dragged all of us to Clarkston's house for one last dinner before we left the following day, and his distaste lingered throughout the entire affair. Briar, Ian, and Avan had planned on covering his home and the town in their wards in the morning, our group taking back off to Eraston immediately after. Ian didn't want to chance the crown taking note of the large use of magic and attempt to come this way. While they wouldn't find Islar, they might find us on the road.

Clarkston had been shifty the entire evening, and I didn't like the skittish way he kept glancing at Briar. She tried to be pleasant with him and engage in conversation, but it was stilted, so she focused on her last night with her beloved sister.

"What the hell is up his ass?" Jonas whispered, leaning over the table. His gaze shot towards Clarkston—I guess I wasn't the only one who noticed something was up.

"I'm not sure, but if he keeps being a dick to Briar, I'm going to drag her and Ainsley back to Eraston," Ian snarked, taking a long sip from his wine glass. We were all on edge, so I tried to write it off as nerves and focus on the witch next to me.

Her hand drifted to my thigh every so often, squeezing in reassurance that I was still with her. I tried not to be overly possessive of her time—I did have four other men to contend with—but I could feel the puzzle pieces of our magics weaving together to form a tight bond.

I knew Avan, Cal, and Ian had threads already connecting them together before Briar, but it seemed like a convenience rather than an actual bond. Now that she was here, they flourished, their magics growing stronger. Jonas', too, if I was being honest. His water magic had been weak from disuse, but with Briar's gentle hand and her powerful magic working with him, he grew stronger each day.

Yesterday had been wonderful, strength coursing through me after Briar left me thoroughly boneless, and I felt as if I could lift a mountain with the energy I had. I shifted the vegetables around on my plate, glancing out the window to gauge how much longer I had to sit here before we could sleep. I was anxious to get Briar back to the safety of Eraston.

"Remind me how often you have to be here to re-ward the home?" Clarkston interrupted whatever Briar had been saying, leaving her mouth hanging open and Ainsley nudging against him.

"Avan and Ian estimate every four to six months or so. We will start with four and see how they hold up before we set anything in stone," Briar ground out. We were all feeling annoyed with Clarkston, so I grabbed her hand and placed a kiss on her knuckles to draw her attention towards me.

"Would you like to go home, little one?" I whispered to her. She bit her lip, gaze darting towards Ainsley before nodding. She began saying her goodbyes and promised to be there early in the morning.

As we walked down the steps to the street, I let everyone pass by before turning back towards Clarkston's home. Ainsley was waving furiously, swiping at her eyes before going back inside. My eyes met Clarkston's as his hand ushered behind her, pure righteous anger shooting my way. I waved my hand in farewell, just to piss him off a little more, and he sneered before snapping the door shut.

What the fuck was that guy's problem?

BRIAR

Power thrummed beneath my fingers as I wove a complicated motion over Clarkston's house. He'd been so strange last night; I could almost hear his jaw grinding every time his eyes darted from Ainsley to one of us. He'd always been so pleasant before, and I didn't want the fact that I had magic as the reason for his sudden coldness towards me.

Avan nudged my shoulder as my magic shimmered away, a soft smile on his lips as he took my hand in his. Ainsley was standing back and allowing us to work the magic, but now that we were done, it was time to face the awful truth of leaving her here.

My arms bundled her into me, and I gave her a watery smile as we said our goodbyes. I would see her again in four months, I kept telling myself, to keep the tears at bay. We'd never been apart so long, and it was a tough thing to swallow.

"Have a safe trip, Bry," Ainsley mumbled into my hair, pulling back with a watery smile of her own. She would be safe here, I made sure of it, so why was it so hard to let go?

Ian was the one with enough sense to separate us, our horses braying and loaded up off to the side. Clarkston grabbed onto Ainsley's shoulders and gave them a gentle squeeze as she waved us off.

Something still wasn't sitting right in my gut at the way Clarkston glared at our retreating backs, but I swallowed the notion and focused on the men surrounding me. We still had so much to figure out. Queen Ameia and the council were still taking the magic of registering witches, and I itched to know why. Ameia was powerful in her own right, living the normal lifespan of a witch and queen of a country to boot. She ruled over her lands with a gentle hand and enriched the economy so that Alehem bloomed under her.

So, why would she need to pull from the magic of the population? If the book Ian and I found was correct, the manna of witches came from the earth. I could feel it underneath my feet every time I walked, pulsing and writhing in the ground like a living thing. It was strong, so there should be no reason for Ameia to pull magic from the populace.

Evin had told me I needed to learn control, and there was a lot of truth to that. I had become so complacent with the random bursts of power, I didn't think of the implications of so much untapped energy flowing from my body. Each time I was with one of my men, the pleasure they wrenched from my body seemed to be the catalyst to explosions of magic. If I could keep that contained, the growing muscle would become even stronger.

Who knows what I could do with a little control? I could possibly appeal to the council—show them I was no danger to the witch population.

I was lost in thought as we meandered down the road, the only noises that of our snuffling horses and their steps. I didn't notice the sharp intake of breath, only raising my head when Jonas grunted from up front.

Our horses were held at a standstill, a thick wall of magic bisecting the road and obscuring the party on the other side.

"Halt, by order of the Grand Witch Council and her majesty, the Queen!" a muffled voice shouted through the shimmering magic.

Evin snarled, turning to Ian. "How could they have possibly found us this fast?"

"I don't know," was the response. "We just left Islar. There's no way they weren't already on their way here." Ian cast his eyes at the group of citadel soldiers spread out across the road. One stepped forward, the gleam of his golden armor shining on the dirt path.

"Captain." He nodded at Evin. "I'm sorry to see you again under these circumstances."

"Likewise, Socha." Evin's fingers tightened against his reigns as he kept shooting glances my way. I could tell he wanted me to run, but like hell was I going to leave them here. I would fight tooth and nail to keep them safe; he had to know that.

Socha waved his hand, the shining magic disappearing back into his gloved hand. He was tall, taller than even Cal, his dark hair shaved to the scalp. His piercing green eyes stood out starkly against his pale skin as they roamed over our group.

"Are you going to come quietly, or do we have to do this the difficult way?" he asked, placing his hand against the sword strapped to his waist.

Magic flared to life around me, each man maneuvering their horses to encase me behind them. Socha sighed, nodding to his men.

Chaos erupted, and I was sure Islar was getting a good view of the fireworks cracking around us. Evin leapt from his horse, slamming his hands into the earth as rock and rubble scattered from the impact, rushing towards the advancing soldiers. Their feet became encased in bedrock, one soldier breaking free and rushing towards Jonas.

Jonas' hands weaved a complicated pattern, forming a ball of swirling water as he shot it towards the soldier. The water wrapped around his head, and I saw the panic flash in his eyes as he inhaled.

"Don't hurt them!" I shouted. There had been enough death and destruction. Jonas let the water fall, leaving the soldier alive but unconscious, face down on the road.

The rest of the soldiers had broken free from Evin's rock and quickly swarmed us. I could see Ian battling against a fire elemental, the wall of his smoky night magic holding back the balls of flame thrown at his head. Cal was working quickly with Avan, their combined power wreaking havoc on the three soldiers they fought.

Cal bobbed and weaved around the gusts of wind shot his way, Avan following quickly behind. As they approached a soldier, Avan wrapped a forearm around his throat, the other hand waving around the soldier's temple as green magic was sucked into his head. The soldier's eyes grew glassy as he slumped over, shutting as he was sent into a deep slumber. They worked like that until all three soldiers were dispatched.

Evin and Socha faced off, and Socha must have some telepathic abilities or was just that good of a fighter, because as Evin moved around him, he quickly shuffled out of reach. I jumped from my horse, sprinting to Evin as he roared at me to stay back.

My hands wove back and forth, smoke unfurling to wrap around Socha. He struggled against it, but I snapped the magic like a rope to bind his arms and legs. The growl he released was chilling, like a feral animal caught in a cage.

"How did you know where we were?" I asked, panting from the exertion. I kicked my shoes off, digging my feet into the dirt and pulling with all my might. The feeling of the earth's magic seeping into me was a relief and eased the ache from spending so much magic so quickly.

Socha looked behind him at his fallen comrades, his face twisting into a grimace. "I heard you say not to harm them, young one, and for that, I thank you. If I tell you, will you let us go, without harm?"

I nodded, much to the chagrin of everyone behind me. Ian would be able to weave his night magic like he had so many years ago on me. They would be sent on their way with no memory of meeting us, other than a few unexplained sore spots.

Socha grunted, straining against my magic, but it held true. He sighed, looking straight at me. "In truth, the council had no idea where you'd all run off to. When Evin didn't report for duty, it raised alarms. He was never late. They checked his office—empty. The dungeons— empty. It was thought that maybe the mind witch had somehow taken his magic and escaped, taking the captain hostage."

Avan scoffed behind us, as if that wasn't his initial plan of escape. I clenched my teeth, pulling more against the raw manna to hold Socha as he continued. I could feel myself burning out, and I hoped he would get to the point soon.

"The council issued wanted posters of the six of you, hoping you were stupid enough to be seen. A few weeks went by and nothing. They had thought maybe you caught a boat to Belmare, content to live the rest of your lives in the sands."

"But?" I prompted him.

"A letter arrived, explaining a group of witches were seen in a small river town. The council wanted us to check it out." He groaned as my magic tightened, my anger spilling out through my fingertips.

"A letter? From who?" Jonas spoke up.

"They don't tell me that, Prince—ah!—just that I needed to take a group of soldiers and check the tip! I don't know!" Socha grimaced, the bindings around his arms pinching the armor into his skin.

"Briar, loosen up. It might've been someone in town." Evin rubbed his hand along my arm. "Control, little witchling. Don't let your anger make you do something you'll regret," he said as he leaned in. I growled but pulled back a little so that Socha could breathe a little easier.

"The letter said you were attempting to place a ward over the town, so the council assumed that was where you'd been hiding," Socha panted out.

There were only two other people in town who knew about the wards: Ainsley and Clarkston. My sister would never put us in danger, and the thought of Clarkston so blatantly throwing me to the wolves made my blood boil. I released a scream, throwing control out the window as my magic made Socha's eyes roll back into his head. He slumped forward as my magic released his body to the ground, a groan from him signifying he wasn't down for the count quite yet.

"That insufferable little worm!" My hands clenched and released, itching with the surplus of magic I'd pulled from the ground. I vibrated with anger, casting a backwards glance towards Islar. Ian murmured over each soldier, the tang of his magic floating in the air as he wiped their memories of the skirmish. Evin and Cal dragged their bodies off the road, positioning them as if they had simply stopped to nap.

My feet stomped over the gravel, shoes and horse forgotten as I all but ran back to Ainsley. I knew something was off with Clarkston. His fucking face as we left should have made me turn around, bundle my sister onto my horse, and ride off as fast as I could. A strong hand gripped me, and I growled as I whirled around to face the man who thought he could stop me.

Avan's face broke through the red haze of my vision, his mouth moving as his eyes pleaded with me for something.

"…have to calm down, sweet girl, you're going to catch the fields on fire," his voice filtered in. Jonas was behind him, waving his hands over a patch of grass to my left, bright blue flames licking along the ground. His water magic doused the flames, but more sprung up.

Avan brought his hand to my face, and I could taste his magic as he tried to use his calming powers. I snarled, flinging my hands out to shove him back. Nothing would cool this righteous anger within me, not if I had anything to say about it. I would decimate Clarkston's home for daring to hurt those most precious to me, I would…

"Briar!" Evin shouted, pounding footsteps eating up the distance between us. His large arms wrapped around me and lifted me from the ground. I kicked back, meeting his thighs as he lifted me higher, pulling me into his chest. "Control, little witch! Control yourself!"

The sounds coming from my mouth were feral, and I felt electricity zapping along my skin, trying to get Evin to drop me. Evin clenched his teeth, murmuring under his breath as rock crackled against his skin, coating him in a thin layer of grounding earth.

Ian popped into my vision, fingers tangling in my hair. "Little bird, listen to me. He will pay, but you cannot go blowing up this town with your anger. You know you would be sad if you did. Think of your sister; we have to get her out safely. I'll even let you get a good hit into Clarkston's face before we throw him down a hole. Control your magic. I know you can."

I panted, groaning as I willed the angry magic thrashing inside me to calm. Ian was right; I couldn't level the town when Ainsley was still inside. The disconnect of my bare feet from the earth helped to slow the swell of my magic, and I panted as excess magic slowly leaked back into the ground. Evin groaned, releasing his magic and turning me in his arms. He set me down so that my feet skimmed the tops of his boots, bundling me close and murmuring softly into my hair.

"That was quite the temper tantrum. Remind me never to get on your bad side" Jonas laughed. I chuckled along with him, turning my face and holding my hand out for them to join in the embrace.

"Let's go get your sister, little bird. Would you like to pick the hole we throw Clarkston into?" Ian asked.

"I think Ainsley should have the honors. If you think that was angry, you should see her."

Their chuckles joined mine as my gaze caught on the shimmering town of Islar, innocent to the betrayal that laced through me.

"Ainsley?" I shouted, but I knew as soon as we had opened the door they were gone. He must have taken her as soon as our backs were turned, privy to what was waiting for us down the road. There was a smell of unfamiliar magic in the air, like Ian's night magic but slightly different.

"They aren't here, love," Jonas said, emerging from the rooms upstairs. "It looks like the place was sacked: clothes everywhere, drawers pulled from the dressers. He took her and ran."

"They had help." Ian sniffed the air, wrapping his hands around an invisible tendril of leftover magic until it shimmered to light. He brought it to his nose and wrinkled his face as he inhaled. "Delani," he gritted out, swishing the magic away from his hand.

"This has the stink of the council written all over it," Evin said as we congregated in the hallway. "Delani wouldn't leave their safety to the citadel guards. I bet they're in Quantil, safely behind the best knights the monarchy has to offer."

I breathed, willing my magic to settle against the rising tide of my anger. How dare Clarkston take my sister? What right does he have to send the council after my coven? How could someone hate that much? How the fuck had Delani wormed her way into this disaster?

"Can you take us to the capital?" I asked Ian.

"It would take a lot of magic, little bird. I would be spent taking all of us at once," he replied, lessening the answer with a quick kiss.

"You know my house is right down the road," Avan chimed in, jerking his finger out towards the street. Honestly, I'd forgotten about the monstrosity, content to block out my time in the wastes and the sentient house from my memories.

Avan rolled his eyes and beckoned us to follow him until we were outside of the boarded-up bakery that served as the home's disguise. It was even dustier than I remembered, and the house creaked and groaned underneath us with the return of its master. Avan ran a loving hand along the stair banister before turning back towards me.

"The council will probably realize we're in the capital when the house moves. We will have to move quickly. Clarkston and Ainsley would be hidden in the castle if Delani had a part in their disappearance. She rushed them out of there; she's getting sloppy," Avan said, turning to us and laying his hand against the knob next to the door.

With a flick of his wrist, he twisted to the light blue color, my stomach dropping as the house lurched with magic. It sucked us through time and space, groaning as it settled into its new home in the capital. I glanced out the window, flying machines still whirring in the sky, banners still snapping in the wind. Nothing had changed, while I felt like a wholly different person.

I made to run out the door, flinging open the wooden slab and racing into the street. My skirts whirled around my ankles as I rounded the corner. I could hear the thumps of my coven's footsteps behind me, and heat bloomed in my chest at the way they dropped everything to chase after me.

I pushed past people crowding the castle, some sort of announcement blasted magically for all to hear. I paid it no mind as I looked for some side entrance, peering around the crowd so my coven didn't lose sight of me in the mass.

"A new age of magic is upon us!" the amplified voice shouted. "A meta witch has been discovered in Islar, her powers sure to bring mountains of prosperity to our lands!"

Now that stopped me in my tracks. Ian huffed as he found me first, whistling to the rest as they poked their heads above the crowd and zeroed in. "Did you hear that?" Ian turned his attention to me. I nodded as I rose to my toes to try and find the source of the voice. The cheering crowd roared in response, banners with a floral sigil snapping in their hands.

I found the platform where the crier was making their announcement, four or five people standing next to them. Pushing my way through proved difficult the closer we got to the gate, but eventually, I was able to shoulder my way through enough to wrap my hands around the bars.

Delani was there, a smug look on her face as she surveyed the crowd, her hand wrapped around the arm of a small woman. Some of the council members were there, Morina and a few others missing from their ranks, but it was the shock of blond curls that snagged my attention.

Standing there, clutched by Delani, was my sister.

AVAN

I could see Briar's magic seeping from her fingers at the sight of her sister on the dais. My eyes snapped to Ian, our heads bobbing at each other in an effort to stave off the inevitable disaster her magic would cause. We would have to figure out how to get into the castle and take on Delani where Briar's magic could be contained. There were too many people outside, too many innocent lives.

Briar let loose a growl, so soft I could barely hear it over the roar of the crowd, but Delani's eyes snapped right to the noise. Her lips curled in victory, a saccharin smile directed right where our coven stood. I froze, my hand wrapping around Briar's arm, poised to whisk her away from the bustling crowd. Their cheers rose as Delani flung her hand into the air, sparks of magic shooting into the sky. It was a simple gesture, meant for the crowds as a sign of celebration, but I saw it for what it really was. A signal.

I moved, not looking to see if the rest of the coven followed, wholly intent on dragging Briar back to the house and getting the fuck out of here. We would make a plan and come back.

Briar's hand jerked in mine, but I held fast. Her sister would be fine until we could come up with a plan to save her. There was no way I'd let go of Briar now, especially when Delani had her in her sights. Another jerk had me looking back, Briar's terrified face filling my vision.

"Faster!" she screamed, gesturing behind her. Dark swarms of night trailed behind our forms—the wyrm wraiths. Their spindly fingers reached for Briar, raking along the exposed skin of her legs as they closed in on us.

I roared, not caring if anyone was around us as I threw my magic out to knock back the wraiths. Their tinny screeches echoed in my ears, my eyes searching behind us for the rest of the coven. The tang of magic in the air had us careening around a corner, my body pressing Briar into the wall behind me.

Shimmering wards peeled from my whispered pleas, wrapping gently around Briar and me. Her panicked eyes looked into mine before catching behind me. I froze, pressing closer to her body as I heard the snuffling of the wraiths behind us. Their hot breath was inches from our concealed forms, the wards only hiding our physical bodies as the wraiths picked up our scents.

My hand snaked up, covering Briar's mouth to conceal her breaths. One wrong sound and the wraiths would descend upon us, my wards too halfhearted to stave off an attack of that magnitude. Her wide eyes locked onto mine, and I slowly raised a finger to touch my lips. I would burn the world for her while she was safely wrapped in my arms. The decision was one easily made, no other option crossing my mind.

I flung my magic out, wraiths in my path collapsing and dissolving into puddles as screams echoed through the alley. Briar materialized beside me, throwing her hands wide as her stunning magic joined mine. One by one, we picked off the remaining wraiths in the alley, maneuvering our way back into the street to, hopefully, disappear.

We'd lost track of the rest of the coven in our escape, but as we tore down the streets hand in hand, the shouts and commotion drew my attention to the trails of fire shooting back wraith after wraith. Pride bloomed inside me as I took Cal in, his back pressed against the others as their magics flew into the surrounding attackers. I blew a short whistle, quickly grabbing Cal's attention. A grin spread across his face as he nudged back to the others, quickly dispatching the rest of the wraiths to get to us.

Manna flew into the air as one by one, our magics finally woven together as a coven, we picked off the last of the wraiths. Pools of blood surrounded us before slowly seeping back into the ground, our panting breaths filling the now empty street.

"What…in the fuck…" Ian's words were cut off as a wraith wrapped its talons around his neck. His pleading eyes were the last thing we saw before the two vanished in a puff of iron-tinged magic. Five more pops sounded as wraiths materialized behind each member of our coven, dragging us into darkness.

Delani turned at our crumpled bodies as if she'd expected us, raising a brow before flicking her magic out to close the door. "Wouldn't want dear Ameia to catch wind of you being here, Jonas darling."

"So, you're the one practicing the blood magic." The obvious stench of iron in the air would've answered my question, if not the dripping stream running down Clarkston's arm. Hatred filled his eyes as he clamped a hand over the cut, his jaw ticking where he stood next to Delani's desk. Clarkston's eyes flicked to Delani, stormy clouds filling his gaze while she smirked at me.

"What have you done with my sister, Delani?" Briar ground out, her breaths coming in pants as she rose from the floor. "And you." She turned to Clarkston. "What the ever-loving fuck are you thinking, bringing Ainsley here?"

"She's safe, as long as you do what I ask," Delani interrupted, raising an elegant shoulder, the movement swinging her short hair against bare skin.

"You are an abomination and deserve to be locked up for your sins," Clarkston growled. I felt my magic rising at the threat, but I tamped it down as Briar lunged towards him. Evin held her steady, and she released a string of curses that would've made even my hair curl as she struggled against his hold.

"She has no magic, Delani. What was the purpose of parading her around the castle like that?" Jonas asked, diverting everyone's attention from where Clarkston and Briar faced off.

"The people don't know that. All they see is a pretty little witch, happily partaking in the crusade of the monarchy. I knew you wouldn't be far behind, but I had hoped Socha would've done the dirty work for me," Delani sighed, resting her chin against her fist, as if we were the most inconvenient thing she'd dealt with today. "Dear Clarkston handed me a boon. All he has to do is give me a little blood now and again, and we're even."

"Let my sister go." Briar's magic began pooling around her at her words, her hands shaking with the effort to hold back. Pure, dark rage filtered down the bond from where she stood. We wouldn't get anywhere if she blew them out of the window behind Delani, other than another chase through the capital.

"Ah, ah, Ms. Gresham. You should know better than that. Magic away, please." Delani moved from behind her desk and stalked towards us. "Now, listen to me. I have worked too long and hard to let my plans for the monarchy be ruined by some green witch with barely any training. What I'm offering you is a proposal, one that will benefit the both of us."

"Don't trust her, Briar. She's a snake," I whispered to Briar, my eyes never leaving Delani. She would strike hard and fast, and a ward is only good if you're paying attention enough to cast it.

"What are you offering?" Briar asked.

Delani stood from her position against the desk and took a few quick steps to her towering shelves of books before plucking one from the stacks. "*From the word 'meta', witches with this power are those who are connected most to the manna of magic. All that is, all that was, all that will be. Meta witches are the rarest of us all, destined to be leaders.*' That's you, right? Your magic is what could fix my problem for as long as I need it to. The monarchy's magic was declining for years before Ameia found me, and my plans have brought forth an age of prosperity unlike any before it. In exchange for your assistance, I will allow your sister to go free."

"How would I help the monarchy?" Briar said, suspicion clear on her face.

"Your magic, of course! We would need to properly train you, but your ability to draw on the basest of our magics would help my efforts greatly." Delani snapped the book shut with a grin. I knew she was insane, but this was taking it to a whole other level. "The earth's magic reacts to yours; it is yours to spin how you wish, Briar."

"Does my mother know about these plans of yours?" Jonas interjected.

"What Ameia doesn't know won't hurt her," Delani shrugged. "She is content in her life of finery and leaves the dirty business to me. Can't you see how the kingdom has grown since I've taken over from your father, Jonas? Our economy has flourished!"

"At the expense of our witch population!" Jonas roared. It was the most emotion I'd seen from the young prince, and even through the fury, his regal upbringing shone.

"Inconsequential. No one is the wiser, and what is the price of peace? A few scraps of magic from witches who don't even notice it's missing? No one will scoff at that when they find out it fuels our crops and puts money into their hands."

"Delani, what you're talking about is madness. You cannot take from those who do not willingly give. I'm sure there are witches who would be more than happy to contribute, but stolen magic is unstable," Ian said. "It's a miracle that Alehem has survived this long without being reduced to dust like Belmare."

"Belmare made their choice not to listen to me and look where it got them!" Delani exploded, her eyes wide and sweeping. "Roderick was a fool, and now Belmare is a wasteland. I won't let the same thing happen to Ameia!"

We were all shocked into silence at her outburst.

"That would make you hundreds of years old, older than Morina. Belmare was lost because of a sandstorm centuries ago, King Roderick along with it. Are you saying you were there?" Evin said.

"Of course, I was there. Who do you think was in Roderick's ear the whole time?" Delani scoffed. "He was a godsdamned fool, and Belmare suffered for centuries because of it. Alehem is different, Ameia is different, and you can help us make this land flourish like never before!"

Clarkston shifted beside Delani, his eyes narrowing at her outburst. *If he was as staunchly against magic as I thought, maybe we could work this into our favor.* Blood still flowed between his fingers—Delani could've easily healed him by now. *She was toying with us all.*

"*Briar.*" I floated my magic along our bond, tapping at the walls of her mind. "*Back down. Tell her you'll think about it. Clarkston is not on board with her plan, and we can manipulate his anger towards witches to be directed at Delani. We can save your sister, but we need time.*"

Her head shifted infinitesimally towards me, acknowledging my words before she shot her gaze shot towards Clarkston, anger flaring to life.

"Will you let me consider it?" Briar spat out. Delani wobbled her head back and forth, attempting to think about it for a moment.

"Absolutely not." Clarkston stepped forward, spitting the words through his teeth. Anger rolled off him in waves as he stepped towards Briar before Delani's hand snapped out to stop him.

"Silence," she commanded loudly.

"I won't let her corrupt her sister any longer, witch. We drew her out and you have her. Now, give me Ainsley and leave us in peace," Clarkston roared.

Delani's magic flared to life, her eyes lighting from within as her smile twisted into something sinister. I could feel it before it happened, my words too slow as she shot a burst of her magic into his chest.

Clarkston's eyes widened as the magic traveled through his body, turning each vein and artery a hot, white light. Delani's magic was powerful, Clarkston's body rising with the energy coursing through his body.

"Stop! Delani, stop!" I cried out, magic rolling between my fingers as I tried to throw a ward around Clarkston. I wasn't going to be fast enough, Delani's magic already taking hold.

Briar threw her hands out wide, fingers splayed as her magic threw itself out, encasing Delani in a swirling orb of darkness. Clarkston crumpled to the ground, unmoving, as Delani pounded her fists against Briar's magic.

Cal and Jonas rushed forward, pulling Clarkston's body away from the angry, lashing magic. I worked my magic along with Briar's, our combined strength fortifying the ball containing Delani. I gritted my teeth against the pushback she threw against us, sweat dripping along my forehead. Briar screamed, dark magic pulsing from her hands as she took a step towards Delani.

"Get them out!" Briar rasped, her own magic draining quickly. She hadn't worked with it long enough to develop her control and was spending it too fast.

"We aren't leaving you here," I said. "Get them out, I can hold her. Go!"

"I'm not leaving you here…"

"And I'm not arguing, Briar! Go!" I roared, throwing all my might into my magic, dark green flaring to life as Evin grabbed Briar around the waist, her flailing body snarling and growling at his grip. He nodded at me as he ran through the door. Relief flooded me; I knew Evin would be the one to at least listen to reason. Jonas and Cal held Clarkston's limp body between them, and Cal's eyes connected with mine before they ran out the door. Ian followed behind them, shooting me a harsh look at the doorway.

"Keep her safe," I said, my teeth aching from how hard I clenched them.

He nodded once, and I was alone with Delani. While I had more control than Briar, Delani was powerful and old, and even though I threw ward after ward around her, she broke through each one with ease. I fell to my knees, hands splayed wide as my magic sputtered and failed me. I gasped, hands gripping the woven carpet. Boots filled my vision as Delani stepped forward, her grin practically feral as I looked up. She hadn't even broken a sweat.

"Tsk, tsk. It's not quite what I wanted, but you'll have to do for now." Delani's grin grew wider as she brought her foot up, swinging wide before it connected with my jaw.

JONAS

Briar's screams echoed down the halls as Evin all but dragged her from Delani's office. She tried flinging her magic out, but as her dark swirls met his skin Evin merely flinched as he kept running.

"This way." I flew around a corner, knowing right where the hallway led. The door flung open, the almost sentient castle remembering my magic as we crashed into my old room. It was the exact same, albeit extremely dusty. I'd never allowed the cleaning staff in, content to pick up after myself, and the door would only open for me. It was the safest room in the castle, and we didn't have time to escape without Delani following behind us.

Evin stepped away as he set Briar down, holding his hands up in an attempt to placate her. She was silent, but I could taste the tang of her magic swirling through the room, feel her anger coursing down the bond that fit snugly in my chest.

"I haven't been here in years," I said, trying to diffuse the situation so we could make a plan. We'd rushed into the castle, with nothing more on Briar's mind than finding her sister.

I ran my fingers along the duvet, dust motes swirling into the air. Something tore in my chest as I looked around the room, my safe haven. It was the one place I could be myself. My gaze landed on Ian, murmuring to Briar softly. He caught my stare, a small smile shooting my way. Yes, he remembered this room as well as I did.

Cal and I deposited Clarkston's body onto the floor, and he stirred finally, raising up slowly and taking in the scene around him. Briar glanced over her shoulder, ice filling her stare before Ian drew her attention back to him.

I knew what it was like, what had gone through Clarkston's mind when he made this ill-fated deal. I knew how it felt to be so helpless against something you didn't quite understand, wanting to protect those most precious to you. Again, my stare landed on Ian and Briar, something twinging in my chest as I took in the two people I felt closest to in the world.

My legs twinged a bit as I squatted next to Clarkston. He recoiled before straightening his spine and glaring.

"You're a witch too, aren't you?" he asked quietly, darting his gaze to Briar before landing back on me. "I didn't see you use any magic in Islar, but you're one of them."

"He's the crown prince," Cal rumbled behind me. I jolted; I hadn't even heard him walk up. Sneaky fucker.

Clarkston scrambled away from me, pinning himself solidly against the wall behind him. "What the hell are you going to do with me?" he whispered.

"You're going to tell us where they're keeping Ainsley. We'll get her out of here, then we'll find some dark hole to shove you into." Cal stalked towards him, ever the fiery knight. Flames licked along his hands, and Clarkston's wide eyes zeroed in on the magic.

"I don't know where they're keeping her. They separated us when we arrived and shoved me into that office."

"You're lying." Cal's hand struck, collaring around Clarkston's throat as he dragged his body up the wall to eye level. "Tell me where she's at. Now."

Ian stepped to Cal's side, his fingers hovering against Clarkston's temple as dark smoke magic penetrated through his skin. Clarkston's eyes rolled back, his body going limp. I shuddered at the intrusion, knowing the softer side of Ian's magic rather than the brutal invasion.

"She's with the Queen," Ian ground out. Cal released Clarkston, his body crumpling to the floor with a loud thud. Ian gripped his arm before casting one last look to Briar as his magic enveloped them, and, with a soft snick of magic, they were gone. I didn't want to know where Ian deemed a good enough place to shove Clarkston, what would please Briar the most. She could be as vicious as the rest of us, especially when it came to Ainsley.

So, Ainsley was with my mother. Fantastic.

Briar glanced at me, understanding written across her soft features. She knew what the love I held for my mother had cost me, what it would continue to cost me if we went to Ainsley now. Her face flashed in my mind—my mother's—and dread sloshed through my veins. I hadn't seen her since she handed down my punishment all those years ago, those cold, soulless eyes staring at me.

"We need to hurry," Briar said. "Avan wouldn't have…" Her words choked off, a tumultuous flurry of emotions curling in my chest through the bond. I couldn't untangle what I felt from her own feelings–worry, fear, anger. She straightened, pushing down what had happened to focus on her sister. Avan was the would-be king; his magic would keep Delani entertained for a while. "Avan wouldn't have been able to hold her for long. Where would your mother be?" Briar finally turned towards me, and I could still see the devastation buried under her proud mask.

"In her wing. That's where she stays the most. I guess she leaves everything else to Delani to handle," I said. I could hardly believe that my mother, the woman who single handedly worked with the witch community to unify us, who had worked with my father to implement plans that exploded the economy, was wiling away her days doing nothing as someone else rules. "We should wait for Ian to come back. She liked him."

Briar's eyes unfocused for a moment, and something flared in my chest. I knew, somehow, that Ian was safe and handling Clarkston. An affectionate slither of magic wrapped around my heart, Ian's citrusy scent filling my nose.

"Ian's on his way right now," Briar said. She cast a look my way, knowledge passing between us. Our relationship was so new, but it was rooted in our shared trauma. Briar held her hand out, and a moment later, Ian materialized in a puff of dark smoke, his fingers tangled with hers. "Let's go."

My mother's suites were opulent, just like her. She always had a taste for the finer things in life—dripping with jewels and soft, lush fabrics, a gaggle of servants always in her shadow. So, it was strange when we wandered the halls, only to be met with silence. Not a soul roamed the halls, aside from us, and something dark slithered in my chest.

I could hardly stand to believe my mother had anything to do with this, but by the way she treated me, maybe I didn't truly know her. She had been a loving mother, but when my father died, she changed. I knew she hadn't really loved him, it being more of a political alliance, but losing someone you had partnered with—made a life with—would be devastating. Briar's hand clenched in mine, and I shot a glance behind us to the rest of the group. Cal had somehow managed to procure a lethal-looking knife, holding it tightly at his side, and I looked forward again to try and rid my mind of what we could be walking into.

I stopped our group in front of the large, ornate doors to my mother's conservatory. Loamy smells drifted from underneath, damp earth and lush greenery awaiting us on the other side. I would often get lost in the leaves, sometimes dragging Ian along behind me. Shaking myself, I pushed the heavy door open and stepped inside.

Strained laughter floated towards us, my mother's throaty chuckle following. Briar pulled at my hand, but I held her steady between Ian and me. It would be the safest place for her.

"Oh, darling, you are a treat," my mother laughed, her back to us as we marched up slowly. Ainsley sat across from her, teacup slightly rattling on the saucer as her eyes caught us. She widened them slightly, relief apparent. I didn't want to know what had transpired while my mother had Ainsley in her clutches.

"Ah, Jonas. How kind of you to join us. And you brought friends! How delightful." Ameia turned, her dress rustling with the movement. Her lips spread into a wide smile as she stood and made her way towards me. "I was just enjoying tea with Briar's lovely sister here. Come, come!

Sit!" Her arms swept wide, five more chairs appearing in a semi-circle to surround her chair with crackling magic.

I froze, the geniality of my mother a stark contrast to the woman I had seen during my sham of a trial. There hadn't even been anyone there, other than Delani and a guard, when she struck my magic down in an effort to keep me contained.

Briar rushed from behind me, wrapping her arms around her sister. Their soft cries made my mother's brow furrow. The rest of us made a wide arc around her, and I stationed myself in front of Briar and Ainsley.

"What's going on, Jonas? I haven't seen you in so long! How was your trip?" Ameia asked.

I scoffed. "My trip? You mean the one you sent me on to the dungeons?"

"The dungeons? What? No, you were supposed to be on a trip to Belmare. I've missed you so much." Ameia frowned and took a small step towards me with her hand extended. She clenched it into a fist, holding back from trying to touch me.

"Mother, have you lost your mind?" I whispered.

"Mother or no, Jonas, I am still your queen, and you shall speak to me with respect. No, I have not lost my mind. Have you? Where have you been all these years if not Belmare?"

"You sentenced him to the dungeons, Your Majesty. For treason," Ian cut in, bowing low. Always the courtier, Ian. He knew what flattered my mother, what would make her deflate from how I'd riled her up. "The official story was that he was on a trip to Belmare. However, that wasn't the case."

Ameia scoffed, looking around as if someone would pop from the bushes and claim it all a huge joke. When that didn't happen, she turned back to me, mouth agape.

"Jonas, my love, I would never do that. You're my son," she pleaded with me. "This has to be a joke."

"You were the one who handed down judgment!" I exploded, years of pent-up anger and frustration bleeding out. The air grew damp, my magic uncontrolled and wisping around me. "You, and Delani, and…"

"Delani?" My mother whispered. "She loves you as I do, Jonas. We would never!"

Unless…

"What exactly does Delani's magic do?" Evin stepped up, his gaze caught on me, and I knew. Dread sliced through me as I considered what lengths Delani would go to in order to protect my mother.

"Delani has manipulation magic. She can warp the mind, make you see what you wish to see," I murmured, everything clicking into place. "If what my mother says is true, then…"

"It was Delani all along," Briar spoke up, pushing her sister behind her as the woman herself walked up, a feline smile playing on her lips. Briar's face darkened at Delani's approach, Delani snaking a hand around my mother's stunned body before placing a kiss against her cheek.

"What have you done with Avan?" Cal growled.

"Here." Delani waved a hand, magic rippling as Avan's form appeared, shifting as if he were underwater. "There." Another wave, Avan disappearing. "Wherever I wish him to be. I lost my last bargaining chip, but now I have another, and you will agree, young Briar."

"Delani, what is going on?" Ameia asked, distress coating her words.

Delani sighed, peering down at my mother with a soft expression. "Don't worry, my love, everything will be fine." Her eyes glimmered, and my mother's eyes glazed over, a pleasant smile appearing on her face.

"Everything will be fine," Ameia crooned, nestling deeper into Delani's embrace, nuzzling her nose against the column of Delani's throat. "I think I'll take a nap." With a breathy sigh, she extracted herself from Delani and meandered out of the conservatory. My eyes trailed after her, dread and confusion filling my chest.

"What have you done to my mother?" I spat out from between my teeth. Whatever spell Delani had my mother under was messing with her memory. That, or Delani was manipulating everyone else's minds to her whims. It was disturbing to think that Delani was the mastermind behind most—if not all—the laws passed by my mother. She was the one who sent me to the citadel, to those dark dungeons so long ago.

"Like I said before, what Ameia doesn't know won't hurt her." Delani shrugged. "The kingdom has prospered, and that's all she cares about."

Briar shifted Ainsley to the side, more towards Ian. I shuffled my feet to bring Delani's attention fully on me.

"What is your plan here, Delani? Get me out of the picture and play puppeteer with my mother, and then what?" I stepped towards her. She frowned at me, attempting to cast her gaze on the others. Delani was powerful, but would she withstand an attack from all five of us?

Ian reached his hand out slowly towards Ainsley, Briar all but shoving her sister towards him. I only had a few seconds to keep Delani's attention, and I looked over at Cal and Evin, their bodies shifting slowly into defensive stances. We could really use Avan's warding powers right now.

"It's worked so far. You see how happy Ameia is with how the country has turned out. That's all thanks to me. I learned my lesson with Roderick, and Ameia was happy to hand over the reins."

"Have you even given her a choice?" I asked. Just a few more moments; I could feel the tang in the air of Ian's magic beginning to swirl.

"She doesn't get a choice!" Delani roared. "I'm doing what is best for this country, and I won't see it go to ruin because of you!"

Her magic shot out, but not at me. I watched in slow motion as her magic darted towards where Ian held onto Ainsley, her eyes wide with fear.

"No!" I shouted, throwing my magic out to stop Delani's. It sputtered in my hands, and I started running, cursing the whole way. They had to get away. I wouldn't let her take them, faster, faster, faster…

As Ian's magic churned, Briar and the others' forms already disappearing, I knew they wouldn't make it in time, not without a casualty. My heart pounded in my chest as I did the only thing I could think of: throw myself in front of Delani's magic.

It hit me square in the chest, and I heard Briar's voice screaming my name as I crumpled to the ground before silence echoed in the gardens. Safe. They were safe.

I panted, pain spearing my chest from the attack, Delani's sneering face swirling in my vision.

"That's twice now you have interfered in my plans, Jonas. I won't be so kind this time."

Darkness swirled at the edges of my vision as Delani lifted her hand and shot a stream of magic directly into my chest.

BRIAR

"We have to go back, Ian! We can't just leave them there!" Ian and I had argued for most of the afternoon, secure at his townhome in Eraston.

He stood shoulder to shoulder with Evin, their frowning faces a mirrored expression of stone. They wouldn't budge, not when it came to my safety. Cal had stalked off with Ainsley, murmuring about tea and idiotic witches. I watched his arm drape over my sister's shoulders in a comforting gesture before his gaze turned back to me. There was a hollowness there, and I knew he would join me in our fight to bring back Jonas and Avan. He had to.

"Briar, we went in with no plan and lost Jonas and Avan. I'm not going back to the capital just to have Delani capture you, too," Evin rumbled. "We won't leave them there, but you must understand that Delani is exceptionally powerful, and she has almost full control over the queen. There isn't anything she won't do to further her plans."

I wanted to scream, to rage, anything to get this anger out. We had just formed this tenuous bond, and I felt the taut pull between the two men who weren't here. My chest ached, and I rubbed the spot where the bonds formed inside me.

"What is the point of this tremendous power I have if I can't save the people I care about?" I snarled.

"You got your sister out. Avan and Jonas both have their powers. They are more equipped to deal with Delani than Ainsley was," Ian said.

Damn him and his sound reasoning.

I looked towards the kitchen, where I could hear Cal's soft murmurings to Ainsley. She still hadn't said a word, Clarkston's betrayal slicing deep within her.

"I still can't believe Clarkston would do that to Ainsley," I murmured.

"I knew he looked familiar," Evin said. "I didn't think I would ever see him again, but Clarkston and I were in training together. His hatred was powerful, even then. Witches and magic are something he's rallied against his whole life."

I turned to Evin, searching his face. "Do you think…"

"I think Clarkston truly loves your sister, but your manifestation of magical powers scared him," Ian cut in. "He imagined spending his life with Ainsley, but the threat of her potential magic had him running to Delani. I don't know what she promised him, but whatever it was, it wasn't good."

Evin stepped towards me, running his hands up and down my arms before pulling me into a tight hug. I softened in his embrace, wrapping my arms around his middle. Our bond us tugged affectionately, curling in my chest. I buried my nose into his shirt, inhaling sharply before exhaling the remainder of my anger.

Sighing, I pulled away from Evin and looked towards Ian. "Okay, what's the plan?"

We congregated in the kitchen, intent on asking Ainsley about anything Delani or Ameia might have said to her. She was silent, hands wrapped tightly around her teacup until her knuckles shone white.

"Ains, you know you can talk to me," I murmured to her gently, and as I reached my hand towards her, she flinched, just enough to rattle the cup. I looked at where Evin stood at the door, his eyes soft. He nodded gently for me to go on, and I felt resolve spin itself into my chest. I could do this; I could help my sister.

Ainsley sighed, eyes cast downward, her lips curled into a sneer. "They threatened me. He let them take me, and he didn't even try to help. He just handed me over. I thought he lo—," She cut herself off with a gasp, tears rolling down her cheeks, "I thought he loved me. If someone loves you, why would they do that, Briar?" Ainsley flung her arms around my neck, heaving sobs into my shoulder. I ran my hands up and down her back, nuzzling my nose into her wild hair.

"I think he loves you in his own way, Ains. He was trying to protect you from me, when instead he should've been protecting you from the crown," I murmured into her hair. "You're safe here, with us. I will do anything to keep you safe."

We pulled away from each other, and I felt Evin's presence leave the kitchen, something tight in my chest pulling at his absence. Ainsley and I were alone, and her sniffles filled the silence.

"What happened?" I asked softly.

"You left, and as soon as you were out of sight, she showed up." Ainsley shuddered, her eyes glazing over. "Her magic was–it was so different from yours. It felt evil, Briar, like I would never be happy again. I tried to run. I thought for sure she had come to kill us, but Clarkston grabbed me before I could get out the door. I was so scared." Another tear. I stayed silent, intent on letting her work through her emotions.

"The room she took us to was filled with her magic, crawling over my skin like little bugs, and when she touched me, I felt like all of the color in the world had washed away. She hauled me out in front of that crowd, told me to shut up and walk away from Clarkston, and I just froze, Bry. I didn't even fight her. She seemed happy we were out there, but those things she said? I don't have any magic!"

"I know, I know," I soothed her.

"And then they just shoved me into that garden room alone. I was sure they were going to kill me, bury my body in the dirt there. All the doors and windows were magicked shut; I couldn't even turn the knobs. Then, the Queen showed up. She looked at me, and it was like she wasn't even there, talking like we had been friends for years. I didn't know what she was talking about; I barely heard a word she said."

Ainsley heaved in a breath, gripping my hand like a lifeline. "That… woman, Delani; the things she said about you was horrifying, Briar. She said your magic is the bastardization of what true magic should be, that you should…" She heaved a breath. "Die for it."

Something dark twisted in my chest at the thought, that I shouldn't be alive simply for having the magic I do. I gathered Ainsley tighter, hoping my touch would assure her.

"I'm here, Ainsley. I'm alright."

"But are you? Where's Jonas? Where's Avan?" Ainsley pulled back. I choked up myself, tears springing to my eyes as I drifted my thoughts to the two men missing from the house.

"She took them, didn't she?"

"They saved us." My voice was watery, hollow. "Avan gave himself up to keep us safe, and Jonas…" I choked off, tears rolling down my face. Everything Avan had done, all the bullshit and lies, it meant nothing in the face of his sacrifice. Jonas? He'd spent too long in that dungeon to be captured like that again.

Ainsley took her turn comforting me as I sobbed into her shoulder, crackling cinnamon coating my tongue as I realized Cal had entered the kitchen. I pulled away from Ainsley, looking at him, my breath catching at the devastation filling his eyes. I wasn't the only one who lost someone special to me in that castle.

"Ian wants to talk to us," Cal rasped out. I reached my hand to him, squeezing tightly when his fingers laced with mine.

Ian's steps were quick across the drawing room, his gaze catching on me when we entered. He strode across the room, gathering me into his arms like if he didn't touch me immediately, I would vanish.

Evin was seated on the couch, toying with a loose thread. Ian pulled away, squeezing my hand before whirling to stand in front of the fireplace.

"Right," he said, clapping his hands together. "Rescue mission."

We settled in around Evin, my hands twisting with his and Ainsley's as Cal stood behind me. His hands rested on my shoulders, his touch grounding me. They were all like that, hovering around me like any moment I would disappear into a puff of smoke.

"We need to have a better plan going into this," Evin said. "The castle is well guarded, and we don't have Jonas to guide us through."

"Aren't you a guard?" Ainsley poked her head around me, shooting the question towards Evin. "You should have just as much knowledge about the castle's layout."

"I was stationed at the citadel. I could tell you every inch of that place, little one, but not the castle. I was only there on official business, never enough to know the ins and outs. Not like him." Evin nodded his head towards Ian.

"Jonas and I made a game out of who could find the most obscure spot in the castle," he shrugged, but that dark mask fell over his face at the mention of his lover. "I know every nook and cranny of that place. There's a side entrance that's rarely guarded, but we will need your magic to conceal us again." I nodded at him, willing to do anything to get them back.

"They'll most likely be kept somewhere Delani doesn't think we know about. She has a few of those spaces in the castle, away from the guards loyal to the queen."

"I fear those guards may be few and far between," Cal murmured. "Ameia was acting strangely in the garden. Delani's hold on her has torn her mind apart."

Ian nodded, beginning another clicking pace. "The tower is the most likely place, then. There's only one entrance in and out. The dungeons are too obvious, and Avan knows enough of the guards to figure out which one would be sympathetic to releasing them." The color drained from Ian's face, that mask slamming firmly back in place as he glanced towards me.

"Where is the entrance, Ian?" I asked, even though I already knew.

"Delani's office."

The room was silent, Cal's hands tight against my skin. There would be no way to get into her office without her knowing.

"We'll need a distraction," I said, thoughts swirling through my mind. I would get Avan and Jonas back, even if it meant blowing the castle to high hell.

"They're still celebrating in the capital, so it will be easy to enter the city undetected. We need to get Delani out of the castle and into the streets. I think that's where we can hold her long enough to get in, grab the boys, and get out," Ian said.

"How do we prevent her from coming after us? She's too powerful, and with whatever is going on with the queen, I don't think she'll be of much help," I offered.

"Briar, what do you know of mind magic?" Cal asked.

I shrugged. "Not much, other than a few snippets here and there. Why?"

"I think Delani has placed a powerful charm over the queen, and if we can break through it, then I think it would clear her mind enough to see what's really happening. Ameia wouldn't willingly submit her powers to Delani like this," Cal grumbled.

"Love makes you do crazy things," Ainsley murmured.

I patted her hand before rising, Evin and Cal flanking me as I walked up to Ian. His pacing stopped in front of me. I turned back to look at Ainsley, her gaze cast downward and lost in her memories.

"Ainsley needs to stay protected," I whispered. "I know Eraston is safe, but do you trust anyone to keep an eye on her while we're gone? She's going to fight tooth and nail to come with us, but I can't risk her." Ian nodded, lost in thought for a moment.

"I would trust Isak. He would keep her busy enough to take her mind off things," he said after a moment. I thought to the burly metalsmith, to his piercing eyes and gruff demeanor. "Ainsley needs someone to protect her while we're gone, someone like Isak, who would be able to devote his time to keeping her occupied. Merri has a lot on her plate with the tavern and bar, or I would ask her."

I nodded and sat in front of my sister. Taking her hands in mine, we shared a huge sigh until her eyes caught on mine. "I know you want to help, but the best way to help is to stay here with Isak. Do you remember him?" She nodded, worrying her lip between her teeth. "I can focus on getting Avan and Jonas back if I know you're safe in Eraston. Can you promise me you won't come running after me this time?"

Ainsley straightened a bit, a glint of my strong-willed sister poking through. "Yes."

"That's my girl," I murmured to her, winding our fingers together. Turning back to Ian, I sighed and nodded, accepting I was once again leaving my sister behind. At least I knew she would be safe this time.

The tavern murmured and bubbled around us, my fingers tightening over the mug I held every time someone walked too close to our table. Would there ever be a time I didn't tense in anticipation of an attack? It didn't feel like it.

The men huddled together as I scanned the busy bar, the seedy part of Quantil hopefully hiding our combined magic from prying eyes. Witches and humans of all shapes and sizes filled the room. A group of knobbly sprites sat next to us, and I caught their eyes every so often lingering on our cloaked forms. I straightened before turning back to the conversation at hand, willful fire filling my veins at the thought of bringing Jonas and Avan back to safety.

"Mind magic is a tricky thing, and I'm sure Orin had something to do with this. His telepathic magic is inherent, but with the right amount of training, a witch can harness the mind and bend it to their will," Ian whispered, his inflection rising barely above the din of the tavern.

"If Orin helped her, then the council will surely be involved," Evin noted.

"Not necessarily. There are some who quietly go against the council's edicts and would welcome a change in authority," Cal chimed in. He'd been so quiet, his eyes wandering from scanning the bar to land on me. He smiled softly, and I could feel a tender caress on the back of my neck, as if his fingers trailed there softly. "Morina straddles the line—she's helped us before, and I think we could sway her with the right words."

"We shouldn't have to bribe anyone to help us," I scowled.

"It's not a bribe. Morina and the others don't have enough power between them to tip the scales in their favor, so while they don't outright protest Orin and Delani, they manipulate situations when they can to their side," Ian offered, shooting me a gentle smile.

"Kalina and Orin are the two people we need to worry most about. Their combined powers are what make the council so powerful, and their influence spreads far," Cal said.

I groaned, rubbing my palms into my eyes. It seemed no matter what, there were massive obstacles in our way. We didn't know for sure where Jonas and Avan were being held, and drawing Delani out would be like stirring a viper's nest. There was only one thing she wanted—power. Her control over the monarchy was terrifying, and how far would she be willing to go? We kept skirting around the giant in the room, no one wanting to say out loud how we could bring her out of the castle.

I looked at each of my coven, their brows furrowed in concentration as they tried to untangle the web of our plan. The conversation was low and stilted, no one having a good enough answer.

But I did. It was reckless and dangerous but love indeed made you do crazy things.

I stood from the table, murmuring to them about using the restroom, and made my way through the throng of people. I looked back one last time, catching Cal's gaze as I opened the front door. His mouth hung open before slamming shut, pain and sorrow in his eyes as he nodded once. Cal was willing to do what no one else would, fearing for my safety. He knows how strong I am, and his belief in me strengthened my resolve as I whirled out of the tavern.

I would save them, even if it killed me.

BRIAR

The streets were filled with people as I made my way through the lower town towards the castle. I had to make a statement, something that would draw Delani out and allow the rest of my coven to find Avan and Jonas. Tears rolled silently down my face, but I steeled myself and headed towards the jutting spires in the distance. I paid no mind to the people around me, their shoulders jostling into my frame, one final shove sending me into a brick wall.

I took a moment to gather myself, to gather my magic around me and just breathe. Avan's teachings floated to the forefront of my mind—breathing in and out slowly to dive into that deep well of magic within me. I would need every last drop of it to save them and, eventually, myself. My eyes closed as I inhaled, my mind wandering through the streets of the capital. I could feel a faint tremble down the bond, a soft kiss of winter touching my lips.

Jonas...

They were in the tower, my second sight flaring to life as I surged my magic forward. I couldn't break past the wards, but there they were, in the distance: two small flares of magic in the tallest tower, huddled together. I threw my magic uselessly against the wards, willing them to shatter. The shimmering magic within me yearned to swoop into that tower and pull them out.

I fell to my knees, eyes still closed as tears rolled down my face. I couldn't leave them there; I had to do something.

Rough hands jerked at my shoulders as my eyes popped open to a pair of dark shining ones.

"Evin…" I breathed, wrapping my arms around his shoulders. I could feel him sag against me in relief, pushing my back against the brick behind us.

"Little one, you scared the fuck out of me. I thought you'd run off to do something stupid like exchange yourself for them." He pulled back, sketching a brow at me. Of course, he would know. Cal had seen me leave, would've tried to hold them back for as long as he could until I was finished. But Evin? My sharp-eyed captain? He probably knew my plan before I did.

"I am going to save them, Evin. You can't stop me." He'd effectively caged me against the wall, but I stood tall and glared up at him, daring him to drag me back to that filthy tavern.

Which would've been a good idea any other time, but I digress.

"I'm not here to stop you, Briar, but you can't go alone. Delani would eviscerate you and take your magic. She invoked dark blood magic, and you're powerless against it. Those creatures will tear your heart out and leave you bleeding on the floor for her to dissect. I won't have it. I'm coming with you." His fingers trailed down my cheek, his gaze soft as he studied my face. "I just got you, and I'll be damned if I let her take you from me. We have so many more adventures to have together, Briar."

A single tear trailed down my face. I hadn't stopped to think of the men I left behind, how they would be affected if I was captured. There would be no trails, no court held over my wrongdoings. It would fracture everyone, and I was selfish enough to not even consider it. Ian's dark chuckle, Cal's fiery laugh, Evin's soft rumble…I hadn't stopped to think I might not have heard them ever again.

Huffing breaths trailed behind Evin as Ian and Cal caught up to us. "Bartender'll be upset. We didn't have enough coin for a tip." Cal broke the ice in that wry way of his, softening the despair coiling around my heart. I reached my hand out, his lacing with mine as our foreheads connected. The bond between us flared to life, his closeness soothing my frayed edges. I looked beyond him to Ian's piercing eyes, his jaw working as he nodded towards me.

We could do this. Save them. Together.

True night descended upon us, even the twinkling stars above muted behind rolling clouds. If this were to work, we needed to be precise.

My second vision covered my eyes, alerting me to anyone moving in the castle. Ian murmured behind me, turning us this way and that. We got lost a few times, ending up at a stone wall more often than not, but his knowledge of the inner bowels of the castle were making this a lot smoother.

A floral scent invaded my nostrils as we circled the conservatory, the moonless night covering the plants and flowers in darkness. My hands ran over the wet leaves, feeling my way along as my dark magic illuminated a path in front of us. Every so often, I would hear rustling in the distance, my body freezing as I remembered that damned hedge maze. A soft squeeze from Ian's hand would draw me back into the moment, and I had never been happier to have him behind me.

We heard her before we saw her, white curls floating in the air behind her suspended body in the middle of the conservatory. Ameia's soft breaths filled the silent room, my magic having picked up her signature. She would be our best option for trapping Delani into giving up my two witches.

Ameia was encased in a crystal-like ward, her body floating a few feet off the ground in suspended animation. Her face was serene, a soft smile twisting her lips every so often as she dreamed. The ward shimmered the closer we got, pulsing in time with Ameia's heartbeat.

"How are you going to get her out, little witch?" Evin whispered. He hadn't been with us when I dragged Cal from the void, but he would get a treat now. I grinned at him, remembering the soft words Avan had whispered over Cal's body to dissolve the ward. I checked for any triggers in it before I did so, suspiciously surprised there were none. Maybe Delani was too arrogant to think we would come directly for Ameia, or maybe she was too busy torturing my covenmates to remember. Who knows how often Delani did this, leaving Ameia in suspension while she ruled in her name.

"I won't have a bond to pull from like I do with all of you, but since she's linked to Jonas, I think I can pick up on her magic and trace it that way. Our magics are intertwined with ourselves, our inner part of us, like a soul. If I can find where Delani has sent her mind, I can bring her back." My voice lowered, fearful of Delani hearing our plot.

Ameia was strong; she had to be to rule the kingdom. If Delani were indeed as old as she claimed, though, her magic would be more than enough to entrap the Queen. Ian and Cal stood beside me, and I used their calming energy to center myself. Darkness encased me as I broke through the ward, Ameia's body slowly floating to the ground. A rushing sound filled my ears as I dove into myself, tugging along the bond until a faint whisper of winter filled my senses. I tugged along the icy thread, finding myself in a field of wildflowers. It was much easier to find her when Ian wasn't meddling, and I chuckled softly as I peered around the scene.

Bright sunlight filtered down through gentle clouds, illuminating the Queen as she stood in the middle of the waving flowers. Her face was serene, tilted up to capture the warm light.

"Your Majesty?" I called. My steps were muted, everything here a facade of peace. There was a faint undercurrent of fear that nipped around my ankles, fighting for a chance to break through the haze.

Ameia hummed, finally turning towards my approaching figure. Her brow creased in confusion as she took me in, and the wildflowers fizzed in and out of existence before her face regained its calm composure.

"Hello, dear. Who are you?" she asked, her voice breathy.

"My name is Briar. I'm your son's covenmate. Jonas?" I reminded her when she looked confused.

"My son is long dead, my dear, so that is impossible." Pain flicked across her face in remembrance, the lies Delani spun breaking through. "I am here to heal, and I was doing a fine job until you came to pester me."

"Jonas is very much alive and well, Your Majesty, and he misses you. Will you come back with me? We can save him together." I reached a hand towards her, willing the Queen to see this field was anything but healing. She couldn't properly process the supposed death of her son, only mask the pain and suffering she felt at his loss. I could feel the ache echoing through the fields, seeping up through my feet to sour the magic within me.

"You lie," Ameia hissed, whirling on me. Her magic crackled under her skin as she raged. Flowers wilted around her feet, clouds converging in the sky as darkness eclipsed the sun. Panic strummed through me, and I stumbled over my feet in retreat, but as she approached me, it was like a snap and the sun was back. The flowers were perfect again, and Ameia was back in the same spot, sunning her face.

The scene reset, suppressing Ameia's tragedy. She wasn't able to process her trauma here in this alternate reality, and it boiled over so often, it seems Delani built a trigger system to reset Ameia's mind when she went into a rage. I had to get her out of here.

"Queen Ameia?" I lowered myself in front of her, my skirts fanning out over the flowers around us.

"Hello, dear. Who are you?"

I had to think fast -- how do I get her to come with me? Telling the truth wouldn't work; it would only send her into a spiral, setting us back to square one.

"I was sent here by your consort, Delani. There is an urgent matter she wishes to discuss with you," I lied.

Her brow furrowed for a moment before she spoke again. "You are not the usual lady she sends."

"She asked me to come because I can transport us right to her, Your Majesty," I said, bowing low again and hoping she couldn't see the lies on my face.

Ameia hummed, her eyes closing for a brief second again before she waved for me to rise. She held her hand out expectantly, and as our hands clasped around each other, darkness swallowed us whole. I felt a tender lick of flame along my body and used Cal's thread to bring us back to the conservatory.

Our eyes opened at the same time, mine with hesitancy and hers with confusion. I let Ameia get her bearings for a moment before helping her from the ground. Her curls were a mess on top of her head, sticking out at all angles as she smoothed a hand over them, taking us all in.

"What is the meaning of this?" she murmured. "Where is Del-"

"Your Majesty," Ian cut in, bowing low. "There is something we must speak urgently with you about."

"Ian, good to see you again. It has been too long, since…" Ameia cut herself off, sniffing loudly. She still thought Jonas was gone. "Tell me what's happening."

"Is there somewhere more private we can talk?" Evin asked, skirting his eyes to and fro, as if Delani herself would jump from the foliage. I grabbed his hand, steadying myself as I squeezed.

"What's going on?" Ameia's voice rose a bit, her spine straightening. Fire sprang to life behind her eyes, and she made to push past us. I stepped in front of her with raised hands, hoping she would listen to reason.

"Your Majesty, we have troubling news regarding Delani and your son. I think it would be best if we speak with you in a private room. There are ears everywhere."

"Then speak plainly, if that is so, maid," the haughty queen returned.

I cast a pleading glance towards Ian as he nodded for me to go on. "My Queen, Delani has concocted a plan detrimental to the kingdom, and she…"

"I said speak plainly, girl. Your roundabout way of speaking is only making me angry," Ameia said.

I blanched. "Your Majesty, Delani has lied to you. Jonas is alive. He was kept in the citadel dungeons and Delani told you he died. She has been using mind magic on you for her own gains—to steal magic from the witches of the kingdom. She has lied for years, telling you lies about Abel, where she came from, everything."

"And what proof do you have?" Ameia asked, a flicker of uncertainty breaking through her regal mask. The small hope of her son still being alive would be the key to unraveling all Delani's lies. If we can just get Jonas in front of his mother, she would have to believe us.

"Jonas and another of my coven are being held in the highest tower of the castle. I can show you." I held my hand out for her, throwing the lifeline out into the churning uncertainty of a stormy ocean. All she had to do was grab on.

Ameia hesitated, staring at each of my coven behind me before focusing back on my outstretched hand. "How do I know you're not an imagining of my enemies? Sent here to waiver my trust in my lover?" she asked, taking a small step back.

Ian stepped to my side. "My Queen, you know the relationship your son and I have. I believed Delani's lies too, that Jonas had perished in the sands of Belmare. I was guilt stricken for years, thinking I could've saved him. Briar is the one who brought him back to us, willful spirit that she is. She wouldn't leave him in the dungeons and has enveloped him into our coven as if she'd known him forever. I wouldn't lie to you, and Briar isn't lying either. Please, for Jonas and Alehem, will you at least come with us to see for yourself?"

Ameia was rooted to her spot, indecision clear as day across her face while she mulled over Ian's plea. I didn't want to force her, that would do us no good. She had to want to believe her son was alive, and once she saw him, then the rest of Delani's lies would be clear as day. We just needed her trust.

"Show me," she muttered finally, clasping her hand in mine.

My magic rushed out, deep black tendrils wrapping around us and spearing my consciousness directly into Ameia's. Flashes of memories sang between us—Jonas' smile at me in Ian's kitchen, how his hand felt in mine to keep me tethered inside the dungeons, our conversations about anything and everything. The taste of icy winter permeated the entire exchange, the bond between Jonas and I ringing out until it pulled taut. Delani's face swam in, her lips twisted as Ameia handed down my judgment, Ameia's floaty voice as we rescued Ainsley, one last glance at Jonas as we transported away.

Faster and faster, everything that happened since Ian found me in my dress shop flew by, colors of memories blurring together until suddenly, it stopped. Nothing but ebbing blackness and our gasping breaths were left. My magic was drained, slowly sliding back into me as I brought Ameia back to the present. Her eyes were wide as she stared, the queenly mask gone.

"So, it's true," she gasped out. I nodded, still breathless from the quick expenditure of my magic. Ameia saw it all: Jonas' confession in the dungeon about how his father died, how Delani has been manipulating them all for years. Everything I knew, she did, too.

"Unfortunately, it is."

She nodded once before clutching her skirts and rushing past us.

I cast a glance at my coven before taking off after her. Our footsteps pounded along the marble floors, guards flabbergasted as they saw their queen sprinting up the stairs and through the halls. We had to move quickly, before one of them alerted Delani.

Ameia's skirts billowed behind her as she took the stairs two at a time, up to the tower where I'd spotted Avan and Jonas' forms. The guard outside the door was half dozing when she stalked up to him, myself and my coven panting behind her.

"Open this door at once," she commanded. The guard snapped to attention, looking wary before he fumbled with the keys on his hip. The door finally clicked open, and the taste of magic filled the air. A shimmering ward surrounded the door, a glossy bubble keeping the occupants inside.

White curls and bright blue eyes met our party, and Jonas walked towards the door with an awestruck look. His hand met the shimmering ward right where his mother laid hers. Tears poured from them both at the bittersweet reunion. Avan was just behind him, his bright eyes locked on me. A small smile tipped his lips up as he took a step to stand next to Jonas.

"Remove this ward immediately," Ameia demanded, whirling on the guard.

He took a step back from the irate monarch, stumbling over his feet and words. "I-I cannot Your Majesty. Only Consort Delani can remove it, per your instructions."

"My *instructions?*" she screeched. Ameia's magic crackled in the air as she swirled upon the ward, a blast of magic shooting from her fingertips. Jonas and Avan scrambled backwards, arms thrown over their faces to block the mighty light blaring from her.

Ameia's teeth clenched so hard, I could almost hear them crack, but it wasn't her teeth that splintered: it was the ward. A thousand shards of powered light shimmered to the ground as Ameia's magic broke through Delani's.

She rushed forward, all flowing gowns and heaving sobs as she wrapped Jonas tightly in her embrace. His eyes caught mine over her shoulder, a teary smile shot my way as I ran towards him and Avan.

"Oh, sweet girl. I knew you'd come back for us," Avan murmured into my hair as his arms wove around my body.

"Always," I whispered back.

Ameia and Jonas broke apart, their hands separating slowly as he wrapped his arms around my shoulders. "Thank you, Briar," he whispered before placing a kiss in my hair.

"Enough of the theatrics, we have work to do." Ameia straightened, glancing backwards towards the door to Delani's office. We'd been lucky she'd been otherwise occupied when Ameia raced our group through the halls, but our luck would soon run out. "Follow me."

EVIN

Delani was nowhere to be found. The Queen rallied her guards to search the castle, summoning the council to Quantil to hold her court. Orin was missing from the meeting, his absence not going unnoticed.

"There has been a grievous misunderstanding in the years of my rule," Ameia announced. "Delani has fooled you all, using mind magic to hold me prisoner. There is much work to be done to undo her treachery."

I was positioned along the wall, a haphazard guest to her quickly thrown together meeting. Briar was nearby, seated beside Jonas with the rest of the council. Avan, Ian, and Cal surrounded her, their menacing glares shot towards the witches gathered. I was too antsy to stay still near her, so I paced around the room, studying the council and their reactions.

The reappearance of the crown prince was a shock to some, a grim resignation to others. I kept note of the miniscule tells on each face, cataloging who'd known he'd been held in the dungeons and who was authentically surprised. During my tenure as citadel captain, I knew Jonas had been held in the dungeons, but my predecessor told me he was a traitor to the crown. I was too young to question her, caught up in the day-to-day life of running the citadel. Jonas had been relegated to another guard and disappeared from my mind altogether.

I flushed at the thought, that the missing crown prince had been right under my nose this whole time, Briar's antics throwing him back into the spotlight. Her eyes met mine, and a soothing tendril walked down my spine, relaxing away my anxiety. My lips turned up at her attention, and my heart warmed. She would be the salvation of us all.

"...be serious, Your Majesty. Delani wouldn't be capable of this on her own," a council member's voice floated through the haze of Briar's gaze, their cutting voice jarring me back to the conversation. The voice came from a large, blustering man, his face red as he looked at Ameia, rage boiling over his features. His hands slammed against the table as he rose, pointing a thick finger in her direction.

Ameia raised a brow, calm and cool as she responded. "Marc, as you can clearly see, Orin is not here. It is my understanding he and Delani, along with other members of this council," she shot a pointed look at Kalina's smug face, "have concocted this plan."

"A plan that has created an age of prosperity in Alehem!" he roared. Briar shot a look at me, slightly inclining her head. I walked slowly, the man's ire focusing his tunnel vision on others. He didn't hear me as I walked up behind him and shuddered when my hand grasped his shoulder. Marc shot a look at me, paling when he saw my stern features, and wisely sat his ass down.

Briar rose quietly, her soft demeanor catching the attention of the council. Her voice was soft as she spoke. "An age of prosperity that has crippled the witches of our country. Their magic was taken from them unwillingly. That is a grievous mistake, one that needs to be rectified. Delani broke the law and undermined the monarchy by toying with Queen Ameia's mind and wrongfully imprisoned Prince Jonas. She is fanatic in her plot, and while Alehem is experiencing peace now, what is to say she won't bring war in her quest for dominance?"

Her words sent ripples down the council, murmurs echoing through the chamber as they discussed amongst themselves. There would be pushback; I could see Marc shooting glances towards Kalina as the others murmured. Ameia allowed the discourse, settling into her chair as she reached for Jonas' hand. She hadn't let him get too far since their reunion, but his eyes strayed too often towards Briar for me to think he would want to resume his duties as crown prince.

"What do you propose, witchling?" Morina piped up above the fray. Ameia looked towards Briar, whose face flushed a delightful pink as she looked around the room. Her eyes landed on me, and I shot a small smile her way, nodding for her to go on. This is what she needed – not us speaking for her, but for her to realize she can stand on her own merit.

"Delani is a wild card. Her results aren't the issue; it's the way she went about them. I think Queen Ameia needs to reconsider the laws passed under Delani and configure them so they are beneficial to all." Briar's voice wavered a bit but then grew in strength as she spoke.

"And what will you do about her? Throw her in the dungeons?" Kalina sneered.

"Delani will pay for her crimes against the Crown with her life," Ameia spoke up, commanding the room once more.

Briar shot a look towards Cal, his feral grin and chaotic energy coursing through the bond, setting all of us on edge. He was protective of

Briar, and I'm sure he relished the thought of his fire consuming Delani. I shuddered, glad his vicious nature was tempered by our witchling.

"What proof do you have, Ameia?" Marc questioned, shooting a look at my scowl. I wouldn't hesitate to throw his ass out if he had another tantrum.

Ameia looked to Briar, nodding towards the council. We had discussed this previously, but I was still on edge about Briar showing so much of her power. Briar heaved in a breath, her magic sparking in the air as her eyes rolled back in her head.

A dark, swirling mass of magic exploded from her fingertips, forming a large sphere above the table. Several council members shot back from their chairs, a few shimmering wards appearing in front of them. I felt Avan's eye roll more than saw it, as my gaze was focused on the scene playing out inside Briar's magic. It was a more condensed version of what Briar had shown to Ameia, but some of the same scenes played out: Jonas and Briar in the dungeons, his explanation of what had happened to his father, Abel, and how he'd been unceremoniously dumped there, Delani crowing her victory after she captured us, the blood hare and wyrm wraith attacks.

Everything was damning enough to send Delani away for a long time. Just as Briar's magic spooled back into her body, a flash of light drew my attention. Avan and Ian shielded Briar as Jonas threw a hand out to protect his mother. Cal leapt over the table to where Kalina was disappearing, throwing a knife out from his boot. The thud was deafening as it embedded into the wall, so deep only the handle stuck out, Kalina's betrayal casting a dark shadow across the rest of the council.

"I-I can't believe this," Morina gasped. She had always been one to straddle the line between the good of the council and the good of the people, but it seems laying the facts in front of her face placed her firmly on the latter side. Morina glanced to Briar, then Ameia, before bowing lowly. "We were wrong to doubt you, Your Majesty."

Ameia nodded in response, then commanded, "Find her, alive, and bring her to me."

The search for Delani continued. However, we were relegated to the opulent guest rooms of the castle to wait for her capture. Ameia continuously urged Jonas to join her as she fought to regain control of her kingdom. Most guards and courtiers hadn't seen her for years, so her sudden reappearance shook the foundations of the monarchy. People scrambled to and fro, carrying out her wishes. Ameia requested her office be moved from her suites to the main level of the castle, her command center spanning three connecting rooms with stacks of paper, constantly filled with solicitors and lawmakers.

There was a lot to untangle, and she often looked to her son for reassurance. Jonas' sleeves were rolled to the elbow when I found him leafing through a stack of legal papers in his mother's office, his brow furrowed as his eyes skittered back and forth over the paper.

"She's been asking for you," I said, plopping down into the chair across from him.

He heaved a sigh, throwing the papers down and rubbing at his temples. The chair creaked under his body as he collapsed, rolling his head until his eyes landed on me. "I've been neglecting her."

"You have," I answered plainly. The prince didn't like to be coddled;

he preferred us to speak as if we were equals. We were, in a way, our shared bonds flowing from one to another, connecting our magics.

"She's probably furious with me," Jonas groaned.

"Briar is occupied with Avan and Cal currently. I heard something about knife throwing, but we both know how that will end up." We chuckled, and I thought back to the way Briar had pounced on me during a training session, riding my cock until she screamed my name and flowers bloomed in the training field. She had control over her powers now, working until she could hold back the burst of magic that used to slip through her fingers. Still, she couldn't help but show off once in a while.

Jonas sobered, glancing away to the map on the wall. There were starry globs of magic, confirmed sightings of Delani, Kalina, and Orin, spread across Alehem. It was like trying to catch water; every time a sighting would come in and we would dispatch a guard team, they would be gone. I was sure Delani's blood magic kept them one step ahead of the Crown.

"I just want to keep her safe, you know?" Jonas murmured. "I know what Delani is capable of, and every day that passes is another day something bad could happen to Briar. Delani was hellbent on taking her powers, and now she has nothing to lose. What's to say she won't strike again?"

"Us. Her coven is protecting her, and the castle." Ameia had worked with Avan and Ian to re-ward the castle, removing Delani's magical signature from the access points. If she tried to enter the grounds, we would know about it.

"What if we aren't enough?" Jonas whispered as he averted his eyes from mine. The vulnerability he showed was endearing; it often rang in the back of my mind as well. Yes, we were all strong and powerful in our own ways, but what if we separated? What if Briar was taken from us?

What good would our powers do then?

I sighed, leaving the question unanswered as Jonas shifted through more paperwork. It was nice being useful again, my quips and insight allowing Jonas to work through the backlog of sightings. By the way he kept glancing to the window, I was sure his skin itched to get to our little witchling. They hadn't spent much time together, leaving the bliss of Eraston far behind for their respective duties.

"I can finish this up if you want to find Briar," I offered, his hopeful eyes slicing to mine as he nodded. I felt a cool lick of winter down the bond, his magic flaring in anticipation of alone time with Briar. I smiled into my fist, waving as he all but ran from the room. This would be good for the both of them, although I was sure Ian would sniff them out sooner rather than later. His prowling around the castle spooked the staff as he searched for his covenmates.

I could tell when Jonas found Briar, a bright bite of starry sky exploding in the back of my throat in joy, so heady, I felt myself thicken with the secondary emotions. That would be my cue to go, it seems, as I couldn't focus on the papers in front of me. I should have given up a while ago, but there was a gnawing itch at the back of my mind. Something wasn't adding up about Delani's movements, and I felt like it was on the tip of my tongue.

My steps echoed through the empty halls, twilight casting hazy shadows on the various stern-faced portraits lining the walls. Frame after frame of Alehem's monarchy and their immediate families passed, each growing smaller and smaller until I came upon Ameia and Jonas. His father, Abel, stood behind Jonas, their deep brown eyes gazing down at me. Jonas took after Ameia, with their umber skin tone and white hair, striking cheekbones and razor-sharp smiles, but I could see Abel in his eyes. There was a kindness that shone even through the paint, a glimmering mischief I'm sure a younger Jonas reveled in.

A sound drew me from my perusal, the hair on the back of my neck standing at attention as a slither of unease floated down my spine. I hadn't heard anyone walking up, nothing in my peripherals, but there was *something* lurking that set my alarms off. I kept my cool, lingering for a moment more in front of the painting before my steps took me further down the hall.

My pace was languid, even as the tension rolled through my shoulders and the sour taste of acid filled my mouth. It was a familiar feeling as I sank into a familiar routine. Check corners, listen for footsteps or the rustle of clothing…

There. The flap of a dress around a corner. One could write it off as a servant hustling away, but I could see the fine fabric from here: the sheen of fine silk that would be highly out of place on a normal courtier, let alone a servant. I hurried my footsteps, keeping my breath even until I swung around a corner, pressing my back into the smooth wall.

Their footsteps were soft, no wonder I didn't hear them sooner. My breath hitched in my throat as they drew closer and closer until…

A soft exhale of breath was all the noise my follower made as I whirled from around the corner and pinned my arm against their throat. Mischievous eyes glinted as a smile worked up half of their face while a vicious blade kissed against the side of my throat.

"Finally caught on, eh?" A whisper of a voice. Feminine and breathy.

"Who are you?" I growled lowly, holding my breath against the sharp blade pressed against me.

A yank of my hand exposed a bright shock of red hair and a wry smile as I stepped out of the reach of the blade.

"Morina," I said. What in the ever-loving hell was she doing following me around the castle?

"There are eyes everywhere, Captain." She grabbed my hand and pulled me along the hallway, drawing her cloak tightly around herself as she peeked around corners. Down we went, the bowels of the castle consuming our quick steps as white marble gave way to roughhewn stone. Water dripped between the mortar, and moss grew in increasing intervals the further we went. Morina stopped suddenly in front of a blank expanse of wall, the lack of moisture and foliage indicating there was more to the stone than met my eye. She pressed her hand to the wall lightly, pink magic trailing slowly from her fingertips as stone scraped against stone to reveal a hidden room. Inside was sparse, like a safety room long forgotten. There were rooms like this all over the castle and citadel for high-ranking members of the monarchy and council to hide in times of attack.

Morina pulled me in quickly and I withdrew my hand from hers as I rounded on her. "What is so important you had to drag me over hell and high water to tell me. We could've gone to my room or Briar's. In fact, why isn't Briar here in the first place?" I grew uneasy, cursing myself for following her so willingly. All my years of training and I had thrown them out the window. Fuck.

I tensed, my body on high alert. I was strong, and I probably could burrow my way out of here, but Morina was old and powerful. Who knows what havoc she would cause?

"As I said before, there are eyes everywhere, Evin. This place is safe for now, but Orin and Kalina have already infiltrated the castle with their spies. They know of all the safe rooms, but this is low on their list."

"Why are you choosing to help? You've always been a spectator, so what's changed?" I asked as I slowly took another step back from her. My magic buzzed along my skin, primed and ready to strike at a moment's notice. I could feel Briar along the bond, safe and warm wherever she was. If I fell today, I would take solace in the fact she would be well guarded by the rest of our coven.

Coven.

I never thought that word would apply to me, yet here I was, throwing all caution out the window. I had to get to the bottom of what Morina wanted and get the fuck out of here.

Morina sighed, drawing my attention back to her. "There is never a good reason for my actions–or inactions–other than self-service. I am old, Evin, and I don't intend on ending my life sooner than necessary. Orin and Kalina clawed their way into Delani's lap, and while you may think that myself and others on the council haven't taken notice, we have. Xinta, myself, and others who have come and gone know what evils those three have wrought. Some have turned a blind eye, like Marc, but we all see it. The manna of the land is not being replenished as Delani claims; it has slowly ebbed away over time. Her proclamation of prosperity is limited to human means–the economy, peace. Witchkind is failing. Fewer and fewer witches are being born, and those that are? Their powers are a fraction of what they used to be. Taking magic from these witches is crippling our society, and what we will be left with is extinction."

I hissed in a breath, the revelations spinning in my head: witches on a crash course to extinction, helped along by Delani and her schemes. We would be no better than Belmare, a rotting corpse of what Alehem used to be. I could see it: the earth mages of my youth were able to move boulders the size of houses, but now, it took two or three of them to move one. Our country's magic was waning right before our eyes, and no one had stood up to say anything. White hot anger blew through me, and an alarm rang down the bond as Briar noticed my rage.

How could Morina and the rest of the council simply stand by and allow this to happen? Who knew how many years it would take for magic to replenish enough to sustain our kind?

"How does this involve me, Morina?" I seethed.

"Briar. Her magic is unlike any I have seen before, and with each of her covenmates at her side, it grows stronger and stronger. Your magics feed into hers, which in turn, feeds into the land. There was a queen once, long ago, before any of us were even a thought, who had magic like Briar's. She allowed our land and species to flourish, but it is waning. No other meta witch has been born since her, save for Briar. She is the key to fixing everything. Alehem would have been fine if Delani hadn't hatched this harebrained scheme of hers, but she did, and now we must fix it."

I mulled over her words. Of course, Morina wouldn't have been able to bring this to Briar without the chorus of her coven behind her telling her no, but me? My skin itched at the implications. I wanted nothing more than to whisk Briar away from the turmoil, but I also knew Briar. Practical, hot-headed, loving Briar. She would never say no to whatever Morina would ask of her, as long as Alehem and her people would be safe. Briar would burn for those she loved, and all it took was a match.

BRIAR

I sat straight up in bed where Jonas and I had fallen asleep, panic lacing through me. *Evin.* His anger spiked along the bond, but I couldn't place his location exactly. I could *feel* him, Evin's steps winding along the castle.

"Jonas, wake up." I scrambled from the bed, elbowing Jonas in my attempt to race from the room.

"Wh'happned?" He sat up straight, shoving blankets and pillows out of the way as he followed me.

I stopped, poking along the bond until Evin's soft, earthy tones floated to the surface. There was an angry tint to them, rage pulsing within him. I winced at the harshness of the most grounding member of my coven–he'd never been angry like this before.

"Evin's in trouble, but I can't locate him." My dress slipped over my shoulders as I dressed quickly, tossing Jonas' pants and shirt to him before sprinting from the room.

"Briar, you have to tell me what's going on!" Jonas said breathlessly behind me. I wove throughout the castle, blindly skirting around corners as I trailed Evin's faint magic. He'd been in the hall of portraits before veering off into the depths of the castle. Down we went, Jonas' quick steps right behind me.

Evin couldn't be in *too* much trouble. I would have felt it, but something wasn't right. I whizzed past stone wall after stone wall, moss growing heavy from dripping moisture leaking through the mortar. I almost missed it, but there! Evin's magic trailed *through* the wall somehow. I ran my hand over the stone, drawing my magic back inside before casting a glance back to Jonas with a raised brow.

"It's probably a safe room. There are dozens scattered all over the castle for nobility to hide during a siege," Jonas explained. He lifted his hand and shot a zing of magic to the door. The stones scraped against one another to reveal a dark room. A dark, *empty* room.

"Evin?" I called out, stepping into the space.

His magic lingered, as if he had just stepped away a few moments ago. There was other magic here too, tangy and sweet. I'd felt it before, not so long ago in a cave filled with flame and memories.

"Morina was here."

Jonas sucked in a breath as my magic threw out into the room. I wasn't sure what would come of it, but gods, it felt good to release some of the anger. I saw Evin's bond leading deeper through the room, Morina's faint pink trailing ahead of it. Jonas grabbed my hand and pulled me along, weaving his magic through the faint seam in the wall to reveal a hidden door.

Damp air blew my hair from my face, and the musky scent of the streets permeated the passage. Jonas turned and raised a brow at me before we took off together.

What in the world was Evin doing with Morina? Something gripped low in my gut at the thought–had she threatened him somehow? What sort of insane mission would he go on with the most ambiguous council member? Why didn't he call for me?

The passage led out into the streets of Quantil, people passing by the darkened alcove without a second glance. It was dark, night slowly settling into the city. I poked my head out into the street, glancing up and down until it was empty. My magic pulsed under my skin as I followed the trail of Evin's magic down the road, weaving in and around the empty market stands as it neared the river's edge. Ships were bobbing along the waters, the stillness of the night enveloping me in its silent embrace.

"Briar, godsdamnit," a rough voice cracked through the night. I spun around, magic whirling around my hands as Jonas moved himself between my body and the shadowy figures prowling down the alleyway.

"Avan!" I sighed, sucking the magic inside and running towards his dark form, wrapping my arms around him. "What are you doing here?"

He jerked his head back to where Cal and Ian stood behind him. "Ian felt your distress, and Cal pointed us in the right direction. What the hell are you two doing out here alone, and why did Evin let you out of his sight long enough for you to sneak out of the castle?"

I chewed on my lip for a moment, reluctant to drag them into yet another mess, but this was my coven. If anyone was going to understand, it would be them.

Dragging a huge breath in, I recounted the story up until this point, waving my hand in the direction of Evin's dwindling magical signature. "Morina has him, for good or bad, I'm unsure. He is alive, but I don't know what her plans are, or if she's conspiring with Delani and Orin, or…"

Tears sprung into my eyes at the thought as my coven rushed forward, sensing my distress. Cal got to me first, wrapping his large form around me protectively, shushing into my hair as his hands caressed my back.

"We'll find him, little dove," Ian's voice murmured through the wall of Cal. "Can you sense him?"

I sniffed, pulling myself together enough to nod and untangle myself from Cal's arms. I looked to each of them, resolve and trust building along the bond. I could do this. We would save Evin from whatever Morina had planned. My magic gathered under my skin as I cast my second sight out into the streets, darkness enveloping my senses while the dark umber of Evin's magic flared to life.

"They went toward the river," I said, stepping forward and sprinting along the cobblestones. I could feel more than hear my covenmates behind me as I tore through the winding streets to the river's edge. Ships bobbed, the waters not quite still as my path took me to the edge of a dock.

Where Evin's magic suddenly dropped off.

"I lost him," I whispered, magic fizzling into nothingness as I turned towards my coven.

"Are you sure? I don't see any ships on the river, and we weren't far enough behind for them to be out of sight yet," Jonas said, peering into the darkness. His hands wove a complicated pattern, drawing up a stream of water and holding it to his ear. "There hasn't been a ship at this dock for a few days."

Where did they go? I kicked my shoes off, digging into the wooden slats underneath me as I willed my magic to cooperate. I could feel his tension, as if it ran along my shoulders itself. He was…down? My magic flared to life, darkness enveloping me again as I took a second look…and there! Just down a hidden flight of steps at the side of the dock, almost rotten through from disuse and water damage. I ran down the steps, taking care with my bare feet until water began sloshing around my calves.

The steps led nowhere, other than to the river's edge, but there was Evin's magic, trailing along the top of the water.

"Briar, look," Ian said, bending down beside me, grasping something invisible. "Do you see this?" His hand curled around what seemed like nothing, but my magic focused until I could make out a frayed rope in his hands. A sharp tug later had the ward around the dock breaking as the magic disappeared into the air, a pathway appearing in front of us to a cavern hewn into the river's embankment.

We picked our way through the rough rock and moist air, Cal's flame flickering against the walls. Evin's magic trailed along, fresher than it had been on the docks. We weren't far behind them. The air was cloying, the dense moisture from the river wrapping together with the stench of magic. It was overpowering, and I felt myself gagging more than once the deeper we went.

Ian stopped us as we neared a curve in the tunnel, casting a glance back at Cal as his flame snuffed out. There was a pulsing light around the bend, magic so heavy in the air it felt like it was sticking to my skin. Ian moved forward, shadows flickering across his face before he beckoned us closer.

As we turned the bend, the sight that awaited us was one I never thought I would see. A large vibrant orb encompassed most of what appeared to be a large, man-made room. It sang to me, a cacophony of voices and murmurs digging straight to my bones until my teeth clenched from the onslaught. Colored magic swirled inside the orb, casting flickering lights and shadows across the rock, pulsing in time with my heartbeat.

"What in the world…" Avan murmured, stepping closer to the orb. His hand reached out tentatively, his evergreen magic crackling against the warded magic. A snap and Avan stepped back, the orb reacting to his magic so violently, it seemed like the cavern itself rumbled in anger.

"I wouldn't touch that if I were you," a soft feminine voice filtered from across the room. Morina.

She stepped out from behind the orb, carefully picking her way across the rubble, the shuffling of falling rocks clattering and sending the magic into a renewed frenzy.

"Evin!" I shouted, watching as he appeared behind Morina, his face splitting into a wide grin. We crashed against each other, the orb's light flaring to life at our connection. "What is going on?" I asked, my fingers trailing along his face, just to make sure he was real.

"Is this…?" Jonas trailed off, waving a hand towards the orb.

Morina nodded, wary eyes glancing towards the warded magic. "This is the stored magic Delani stole."

"How did you find out about it?" Ian asked, his voice taking on that edge I knew so well. He was about two seconds from ripping me away from this room and taking us all back to Eraston. None of us trusted Morina; she had toed the line for too long for us to be at ease.

"It's a long story. Delani has corrupted the magic of Alehem, just as she did with Belmare. There is a ward around it, which, to my understanding, is different for her. Belmare fell because of the instability of the gathered magic, and she thinks the ward will help," Morina explained.

"But the ward is failing," Avan stepped in. He gestured to the orb, cycling furiously with the magic contained inside as if it was begging to be let out. Along the edge was a faint fissure, small enough that I had missed it at first, but it was glaringly obvious now. Magic leaked out slowly from the crack, which was what permeated the air around us. "We have maybe a few days before this all blows to hell," he continued.

Morina nodded. "Which is why I sought Evin out. I knew his bond would bring you here. I cannot contain the magic, none of us individually can, but a coven as strong as yours would be able to channel the magic back into the earth."

I glanced up to the orb, and the swirling magic slowed, enough for me to pick out a few faint strands of individual magic. The voices swelled and crooned to me, calling me closer and closer to the orb as my coven and Morina's voices faded to the background.

"Come to us, young witch, bright and beautiful, calculating and cold. Let our magics intertwine and flourish into the earth. The destruction of magic as you know it. Let us bring forth an age of awakening, together…"

The voices hissed inside my head, volleying back and forth between a silky-smooth voice and something slithering and dark.

"Come, young one, your magic calls to me, come into the light, come, come, COME!"

Strong arms wrapped around me, yanking me away from where my fingertips almost grazed the ward. A wail pierced through the haze, the magic screaming my loss as Avan spun me around to face him. His arms enveloped me as he walked us back away towards the others.

Avan's eyes flicked wildly between me and the contained magic, his voice soft as he said, "You heard that, right?"

My mouth opened, but a shuddering echo drew our attention to the opening of the tunnel. With flame and wind, Delani appeared, her eyes wide as she took in our company. Her hair whipped around her face as her gray magic crackled down her arms. Delani's mouth curled into a snarl, not wasting any time as she began hurling balls of magic our way.

I screamed as Avan threw us to the side, the magic narrowly missing his back by a sliver. Rock scattered across us as Delani's power ricocheted on the wall.

"You're going to die here, witch," she seethed, her stomping feet meeting the rock in time with the pulsing magical orb. "You're going to die, and no one else will be in the way of my plans. Not you, not your coven, *no one.*"

"Briar, you have to run, now!" Avan's face was twisted in fear, his golden eyes wide and searching as he scrambled us up. "Please. I know I have no right to ask, but for the love of everything, run!"

I searched the cavern for my covenmates, watching as their magics collided with Delani's, their bodies arched protectively around Avan and me. His magic rumbled across his arms and skittered like sparks towards me. I couldn't leave them to die here, not like this. We were supposed to be together, and if they left this mortal plane, then I would gratefully go with them.

Avan's eyes widened with the furious shaking of my head. "I'm not leaving you. You know the prophecy, our powers. We're the only ones that can end this. I…I love you, and I'm not going to run."

I had run for so long, run away from my feelings, from responsibilities, from anything that scared me. I wasn't going to run now. Darkness enveloped me as I drew my powers up from that dark well inside, surging and crackling power running over my body until I lit like a beacon.

The earth shuddered under my powers, my teeth clenched so hard, I thought they would break. A scream erupted from my lips as my power collided with Delani's, wrapping around her in a furious whirlwind of elemental magic. Her mouth opened in a silent scream, body convulsing as my magic tore around her. I could feel pulsing underneath my feet as the rock cracked open, jagged edges rising as Avan groaned beside me.

This *power*, gods, it was heady. It coursed through my veins as I drew and drew and *drew*. I couldn't get enough, my body absorbing and building until I felt like I was going to burst.

Delani's maniacal laughter broke through the haze of magic surrounding me. "Ah, you feel it, don't you, witch? Now you understand. You think yourself so good and pure, but the magic tells a different story."

Through the groans of my coven, I could hear the tinkling shards of the ward breaking as the magic inside the orb fought to break free. Dread crept up my spine – there was no way I would be able to hold back the magic from consuming my coven *and* hold back Delani.

"You will destroy us all," she hissed, seizing as my magic forced its way through her body, so similar to what she had done to Clarkston, her veins glowing like a fiery sun. I basked in the power for a moment, wonder creeping through me as I watched the magic work through her body.

"Briar…" Evin groaned from beside me. My gaze moved to him, our eyes meeting in a furious battle. "Control…Briar…" His teeth clenched hard against the now ricocheting magic coming from the orb.

Control…

My mind was blissfully blank, nothing but swirling emotes of magic threading through it.

Control…

I could stay here forever, enjoying the pleasant buzzing that coursed through me.

Control…

My magic purred as it intertwined with the stolen magic…

That was it, though. This magic *wasn't* mine. It belonged to every witch who had passed through the capital gates, looking for some semblance of normalcy, some reason to belong. Instead, their very life force was taken bit by bit away from them, leaving the witches and land drained of the very essence that sustained us.

"Briar!" Evin called again, oblivious to the turmoil roiling through me. Our gazes locked, and I saw the relief flood through him as I nodded through the haze. This would work. It had to.

Sharp rock bit through the flesh of my feet as I braced myself against the onslaught. The ward was almost completely broken at this point, magic swirling around us in a flurry of rising voices and colors. I plucked and pulled at my magic, willing it to slow the tempest of my body.

A scream tore from my throat as I finally grasped along the bond of my coven, their powers culminating with mine like a lifeline tethering me into the earth. The land sang to me, a sweet lullaby compared to the thrashing chaos of the stolen magic.

"Hello, sweetling, the most precious of us all. Return what was stolen from us, restore the balance. Come little spark and give back what has been ripped from the natural order…"

It was easy enough, giving into what the magic demanded of me, to let it flow through my body and surge into the ground like the conduit I was. It plucked and pulled at my magic, threatening to take what I gripped so tightly onto: my bonds. Flashes of red hair, a scar, a cold winter's kiss, rough hands, all blurring together into one bright, unbreakable thread.

My scream cut off as the magic died, leaving me a gasping mess on the floor. Our pants filled the cavern, and as I cast my gaze around, I landed on Delani, crumpled on the floor. Five pairs of strong arms surrounded me, blocking my view as my coven descended upon me.

"Holy fuck, Briar, that was *insane!*" Jonas' voice filtered through the bodies.

Evin's rough hands cupped my face and brought my attention to him. Something unspoken flowed between us and his lips curled into a smile before pressing a kiss against my lips.

Ian's mask was back, but I could see the relief in his gaze as his hand trailed absently over Jonas' back, Cal and Avan's hands laced with mine before drawing me in between them. A sharp skittering of rock had us tensing, but it was Morina kicking Delani's limp form.

She shrugged, and nudged Delani again before turning back to us. "She's still alive."

For now. The words went unspoken, for the crimes Delani had committed against the kingdom were too great, too horrific, to let slide.

She would be dealt with.

AVAN

"Consort Delani, do you have any last words?"

The magistrate's voice rang out through the courtyard, the crowd unusually silent as they started up to the dais. Just a few days ago, they had been singing Delani's praises, but now, after the quick–and very public–trial, they were quick to turn on her. You could have heard a pin drop from where my coven and I stood near the front, Briar's hand sticky in mine as she held onto me like a lifeline.

She'd been so quiet during the trial, excusing herself from testifying. It would seem those last words Delani said haunted her. Her big gray eyes stared at the spot where the noose tightened around Delani's thin neck.

"You will destroy us all…"

"We don't have to be here for this," I whispered into her ear. Briar shuddered against me, glancing away from Delani for just a moment to shake her head.

"I need to be here for this. She terrorized us, took you away from me, and threw Jonas in a cell. Her actions almost destroyed the entire country. She deserves this," Briar whispered back, strength finally straightening her spine. Pride snaked through me. My strong, beautiful witch. We would weather this storm, together, as it should be.

The crack of the platform and sharp snick of rope were all I heard as I continued looking at Briar. Her face paled, but no sounds came from her lips. I hoped for a quick death, if only to ease Briar's guilt.

I had seen what the magic did to her, those dark, hissing words slithering through her mind. A thread, a simple thread, was the one thing that held her mind in this world from the siren song of the stolen magic. That ward had been hastily thrown around the magic, and it was honestly only a matter of time until it had exploded and possibly leveled Quantil, possibly most of Alehem.

After we had secured Delani's unconscious form for transport, I found Briar running her hand over where her feet had been planted. There were scorch marks there, and the air zinged with the aftertaste of magic.

Her wide eyes latched onto mine, our terror reflected on each other's faces from the enormity of her magic. I gathered her in my arms as my hands soothed against her back.

The trial had thrown our coven into a frenzy, each member working with the Crown against Delani, all except for Briar. Her hollow eyes stared at me from across the rooms as the Crown readied its case against their queen consort.

"Let's go home," I whispered to her, thoughts barreling back to the present as the crowd around us began to stir back to life.

"You have to talk to her."

"You're the one who knows her best, *you* talk to her."

Their incessant hissing was going to drive me mad. I stood from the couch in Ian's Eraston home, effectively silencing the snarking between Ian and Evin.

Ever since landing back in Eraston, Briar had been subdued. Her sister couldn't even pull her from her melancholy, and the small smile she shot towards Ainsley bouncing down the street from Isak's shop was the first glimmer of the old Briar I'd seen since the cavern.

She was sleeping, or at least pretending to, up in her room. Alone. Instead of being with her, we were down here, bickering and arguing. I huffed an eye roll at the idiots still staring up at me and went in search of Cal. Maybe he could be the one to break Briar from her terrors.

His shoulders tensed as I walked into the kitchen, easing once I sent a gentle stroke down the bonds connecting us.

"Hey." Cal shot a soft smile my way.

"Hey, yourself." I kissed his temple before snatching the half-eaten apple out of his hands and munching happily at his cross expression.

"You're a little shit, you know that, right?" he grumbled before grabbing another apple off the counter. "I ought to fill your mouth with something else so I can get a moment's peace."

I felt the heat rush through my stomach at his words. It had been days since we'd seen each other for more than a passing moment in a hallway, and I ached for his—and Briar's—closeness. Their hands, searching and roaming along the tender flesh of our intertwined...

"Avan. Did you need something? You have that glazed look in your eyes, like when you think about me fucking you. I'm sure we could sneak away for a quickie," Cal chuckled, catching my jaw between his fingers.

I huffed and tore my burning face away, crossing my arms. "We have to check on Briar. I haven't felt anything down the bond in days, since the caverns. It's usually a mess of her emotions and feelings, but lately? Nothing. Something is wrong."

He nodded, rubbing at that spot in his chest mirroring mine. Our usually bright witch was dimming right before our eyes. Cal's head jerked for me to follow him, and we made our way upstairs to the room Briar had commandeered so long ago.

"Bry?" I whispered into the dark room. The stars were subdued tonight, the usually energetic town dull in comparison to its usual fervor. I couldn't help but notice it was a dark reflection of Briar's current state. A soft rustle drew Cal and I closer to the bed, where she was cocooned in a swath of comfortable fabrics.

"I'm here," her soft voice came from the bed. A slender hand poked out and patted the mattress next to her as Cal and I positioned ourselves on either side. Briar's sigh was soft, her wavy hair making an entrance before her face popped out of the blankets.

"Do you wanna talk about it, darling?" Cal murmured.

It was silent for so long, I would've thought she had fallen asleep if it weren't for the moon shining its light across her face, gray eyes open and wide as she mused over her words.

"That...*power*. It was unlike anything I'd ever felt before. It's no wonder it drove Delani mad. There was no way she could have contained it for much longer. What would have happened if Morina hadn't stepped in at the stroke of midnight? Alehem would be wiped off the map. If Evin hadn't broken the spell around my mind, what would have become of me? Of you? I was so close to losing it..." Her voice broke off with a whimper.

Cal and I shared a shocked expression over the top of her head. His jaw ticked, and I saw the fire light behind his eyes. If Delani hadn't already been strung up, he would've done it himself.

"It could have been any one of us, Briar. It isn't a reflection on you that you had those thoughts. What matters is that you *were* able to break free from them. You saved this whole city, possibly even the whole country. Fate has a strange way of working itself out, and yes, maybe Morina chose a very inconvenient time and way of going about things, but it happened. Now, we move on as best as we can. Together," I said to her. Pleasantries wouldn't get far with Briar, and she appreciated the truth most of all. I had learned that the hard way, and I wasn't going to make the same mistake again.

Her eyes grew watery as she looked up to me, so small inside the fortress of comfort surrounding her. I plucked and peeled the fabric from her body until she sat before me. Her face felt like heaven as I took it into my hands, forcing her to meet my gaze fully.

"You will get through this. It will get better. You did everything right, Briar. I couldn't have asked for anything different," I said firmly. "Do you understand me?"

Her eyes darted to the side, her lip caught between her teeth as she anxiously gnawed at the soft flesh. I thumbed her lip from its trap and placed a soft kiss against the redness spreading from her ministrations.

My gaze softened as our foreheads touched. "We're all here, together and safe, for probably the first time in a long time. I will move heaven and earth to make sure it stays that way, hmm?" Briar's face nodded in my hands before she leaned up for a kiss.

Honestly, I really tried to keep it light. I didn't want to overwhelm her after the whirlwind of emotions she'd been experiencing, but damn, she tasted too good. Briar's tongue swiped against the seam of my lips with a hesitant question, and I obliged her willingly.

Briar and Cal moaned at the same time, sending a zing of electricity straight up my spine as I deepened the kiss. This was exactly where I never thought I would be, all those lonely years building up walls to keep people out, especially ones who meant so much to me. I lied, kept secrets, and twisted the world in order to keep myself safe.

That all changed when Briar blew into my life. She broke down those walls brick by brick until she saw the person underneath, and she never gave up. That kind of love is so rare, and I spurned it so hard. I didn't see the people in front of me who made up my whole world—Cal and Briar. The others in the coven were…*fine*. Evin, Jonas, and Ian made Briar happy, and while we all constantly annoyed the shit out of each other, we all worked.

This family was something I wasn't going to give up willingly, and I was going to make Briar see that until my last breath. An idea formed in my head, one that would take one last teensy manipulating scheme, but it would be worth it in the end.

Briar's soft lips sighed against mine before she pulled away at last. Cal sandwiched her between the two of us, his hands roaming gently up and down her body until she shivered with anticipation. The fabric of her shift bunched in his hands as he peeled it off her slowly, exposing her heaving chest and glazed eyes.

"I…I…" I started, staring into those gray orbs as something bloomed in my chest, something I had never told another person, not even Cal, even though I had felt this way for a long, long time. I glanced over Briar's shoulder to Cal, his hands stilling against her stomach while his chin rested against her shoulder. I could do this.

"I love you. *Both* of you. Cal, I've loved you ever since you dragged me from that library. Your fierceness and ability to see through my bullshit is something I admire, and your ability to love without abandon is the best part about you."

"I'm sure there are other parts that are the best," he scoffed quietly, eliciting a soft giggle from Briar before they focused back on me. I rolled my eyes to the ceiling before continuing.

"Briar, I know I have a lifetime to make amends with you for the way our relationship began but know I will do everything in my power to make sure you are happy and safe and free from the constraints of secrets kept. You complete us in a way I never thought would be possible, but here you are, fitting perfectly in the puzzle of our lives like you were made for us." I accentuated my speech with a long kiss for each of them before pulling back, utterly vulnerable.

Cal stared at me for a beat before kissing Briar's temple and whispering something in her ear that made her eyes go wide with excitement. It was the first real emotion she'd shown since the cavern, and I was elated the true Briar was beginning to peek back from behind the curtain she'd drawn around herself. Briar nodded before tackling me against the bed, straddling her thighs around mine and pinning my hands above my head.

"I love you too, Avan. So much." Briar kissed me long and languid, taking her time to explore my mouth. "Cal says I should make you squirm, and I quite like that idea."

My gaze flicked to Cal, his salacious grin appearing behind Briar's back before nodding back at Briar. Her grin was infectious, and I felt the slither of her magic tighten against my hands, holding me securely against the headboard.

Briar bent forward, kissing and licking along my jaw and throat before unbuttoning my shirt and placing soft kisses against the curls of my chest. Cal tugged and pulled at my hands, lifting my hips with ease as he divested me of my garments, leaving me hard and exposed to the chilly air. Briar lifted, snapping her fingers and, with the taste of magic on the air, my shirt—along with Cal's outfit—disappeared into thin air.

"Ian's been showing you his tricks," I breathed, straining against my bonds. They were weak wards, and I could break through them easily, but that was the point of this little game, wasn't it? Control. I easily handed the reins over to Briar, knowing she craved this as much as I did.

"Among other things." She grinned before lifting so Cal could replace her. His length surged forward into my face and my mouth watered at the sight. I opened willingly as he slipped between my lips, the sweet tang making me moan around him. Cal pumped slowly, opening my mouth wider and wider until his hips met my mouth, and I swallowed him whole.

"That's it, my love," he groaned. "Take it all like the good boy I know you are."

Pleasure thrummed through me at the praise, unlocking something in me I *definitely* wanted to continue exploring.

Briar's hands skimmed along my thigh, just missing where I ached for her to touch. Cal inside me had heat coursing through my veins, and I knew if she even ran her fingers along my cock, I would explode.

Cal's hand ran along my jaw, pinching against my chin as he tilted my head up so our eyes locked. "You look so good with my cock in your mouth, Avan. Doesn't he look pretty, darling?" he asked Briar.

She hummed in agreement, soft kisses trailing along my thighs as she skirted around my hips in a way that had me thrusting and bucking into the air uselessly. "He does, darling, but it seems like he's missing something, doesn't it? What could that be?"

Briar's fingers skimmed over the base of my cock, and I let out a moaning scream around Cal. I was so hard, it was almost painful, until her hot mouth closed around me, and I saw stars. Cal withdrew from my mouth until my lips curled around his tip before slamming back in. The duality of Briar sucking me and Cal thrusting into my mouth in an alternating pattern was heady.

Magic began crackling against my skin as I soared higher and higher, almost to the peak, and I was sure I would float away into the ether a happy man.

Everything stopped at once. Cal and Briar drew away almost simultaneously off the bed, leaving me panting and achingly alone.

"Ah, ah," Cal admonished, drawing Briar close until her back pressed against his front. "You don't get to come until we do, selfish thing." His hands skirted her hips and waist, grasping Briar's heavy breasts in his hands and kneading until she squirmed against him.

Briar reached behind her, grasping Cal's length firmly and stroking up and down, taking my spit and coating him in wetness. He groaned into her hair before wrapping a hand around her throat, tilting her head until their lips met in a crushing kiss. I couldn't touch them or myself, and my wrists strained against Briar's magic, my hips bucking uselessly into the air. I craved the warmth and friction of their bodies.

"Magic above, you two are perfect," I groaned.

Briar smirked at me before Cal bent her over the edge of the bed, her mouth so close to my cock that her puffs of breath made me whine in frustration. Cal's hand wrapped around Briar's hair and arched her back, drawing that hot heat away from me.

"*Fuck*, Cal, please!" she moaned as his other hand skated along her back, her squeal as his palm cracked across her ass pushing me closer to the edge. A bead of wetness pooled at the tip of my cock, dribbling down my length at the sight.

Cal smacked Briar's other cheek before surging into her, their shared groans echoing mine as he began furiously pounding into her. I could only watch as Briar shattered around Cal's cock, the buildup of our joining cresting her over the peak of ecstasy as quickly as it began.

"Who do you belong to, darling? Whose cock do you take so well? Whose dripping pussy is this?" Cal gritted out, his words punctuated with his thrusting hips.

"Ohhh, yours! It's yours!" Briar moaned out, shivers wracking her body as another orgasm crashed through her.

"That's right." Another crack and more redness bloomed across her ass. "This is ours, darling. You're ours." Cal let go of Briar's hair and her head drooped back to my hips. I stilled myself, still fully engrossed in this teasing game of theirs, but her lips sought refuge against the tip of my aching length.

Briar licked that bead of wetness back up, sucking the whole tip into her mouth before she bobbed up and down in time with Cal's thrusts. Heat coiled in my gut before working its way up my spine. Cal's earlier words echoed in my mind as I breathed through the sensations, holding myself back.

"Gods, you're both aching for this, aren't you?" Cal murmured. Briar and I nodded at the same time, and a flash of heat crossed Cal's piercing gaze as he picked up his pace. The slaps and slurps echoed through the room before Cal's face twisted into that familiar growl, a sign he was about to come undone.

My release spilled down Briar's throat as she convulsed around me, Cal's roar piercing through the stars that dotted my vision until we collapsed against the soft down of the bed. Briar's magic disappeared, and my hands met her sweaty face before pulling it to meet mine in a soft kiss. I could taste myself in her mouth, and my cock stirred uselessly. I was utterly spent.

Cal drew us all back into the comfy nest Briar had built for herself, dragging the blankets around us until we were all cocooned together.

"I–" Her yawn interrupted her words, "love you two. So…much…" Briar's voice dragged off as sleep overtook her, a peaceful look on her soft features instead of pinching worry.

Cal stroked a hand along her hair before he grabbed my chin between his fingers and dragged my gaze to his. It was silent for a moment as we stared at each other before his lips parted.

"I do love you, Avan, you infuriating man. I'm a little annoyed it took you this long to come to this conclusion, but I am happy you did." Cal's words were softened with the kiss he gave me, and the heated look that took over his features had me wanting to wake Briar up and go for round two.

"Enough of that. We need to let her sleep. There's always tomorrow." Indeed, there was.

BRIAR

Six months later…

The capital still bustled along, innocent as ever. The dark undercurrent of Delani's exploits was gone, and magic had flourished. The street performers' magic when Avan first brought me here was dim in comparison to the sights I saw now.

Jonas' hand curled in mine as we made our way down the street. Evin protested us going together alone, but when Jonas threw a spiraling current of water to pin Evin down, he finally relented. Jonas' grin was wide as I whirled us back to Quantil the next day.

"This place is never dull, eh?" Jonas asked as we watched a troupe of witches, their shadow magic miming a play against the stone facade of a building for the gathered youngsters.

The shadow dragon roared mightily, an elemental witch shooting out a stream of molten fire, as if the shadow were breathing and living. I giggled along with the children. "Never a dull moment."

Queen Ameia had requested my presence in Quantil to sit in

on her newly formed parliamentary oversight committee. She still suffered from flashbacks, and her rule was thrown into question. However, instead of replacing her, it was decided Alehem would move to a more equal decision-making process between witches, humans, and the monarchy.

I was pleased to have Jonas and Avan all to myself, in addition to Cal, Evin, and Ian, and I could admit I wanted as little to do with the monarchy as I possibly could. Still, Ameia was still Jonas' mother, and another big reason for us coming to Quantil. Jonas missed his mom.

Inside the castle, not much had changed, except for the bustling epicenter that was Queen Ameia's office. Workers poured in and out of the large oak doors, papers hovering in mid-air in front of them.

"Jonas!" Ameia's delighted voice carried over the hustle and bustle of her worker bees. Her arms clasped around her son in a tender embrace before moving to me. I had found that the Queen, when not under Delani's spell, was quite affectionate.

"Mother, you know you can take a break once in a while. That's what the committee is for," Jonas admonished. Ameia shooed away his worry before dragging us out into the hallway.

"I have lunch arranged for us at high sun in the conservatory. Please don't be late, my love. You know how cranky I get when you're late." She toed up to give her son a kiss on the cheek and patted mine affectionately before whirling back into her office.

"It seems we have some time to kill." Jonas eyed me, grinning as he tugged me along the familiar hallway. His door opened of its own accord as Jonas dragged me inside, twirling me around before pinning me against the now closed door.

Magic. Amazing.

His lips met mine in a blistering kiss, his hips thrusting into mine and pressing me even further into the carved wooden door.

"I was thinking we could do some embroidery," Jonas murmured against my lips, his hands grasping at the hem of his shirt and pulling it over his head.

"Oh, I was thinking about taking a perusal around the library. I hear there are some very *thick* books there," I giggled, kicking off my shoes and pulling at the strings of my dress as the silk fluttered to the floor.

"What about taking a stroll around the courtyard? I would hate for all this beauty to go to waste." Jonas stood in front of me, fully naked, as his gaze raked over my bare skin. I flushed at his attention, still in awe that I had five gorgeous men who worshiped me like a goddess. There wasn't a day that went by that one of them wasn't pinning me against some surface or another, feeding me mouthfuls of cock or strawberries. It honestly depended on the time of day.

I tapped a finger against my lips as I hummed, sidestepping Jonas before walking backwards into the room. This was what I loved most about Jonas: his playful manner and the way he made me laugh. I knew when Jonas and I came together, it would be filled with giggles and teasing touches as much as moans and thrusts.

"I feel a bit too chilled to walk around the courtyard. Ian would probably have a fit if he saw us outside like this. We wouldn't want to piss him off, hmm?" I asked as I sank into his bed. His room was much cleaner now that we came to the capital more often, and the sheets had been freshly changed for our arrival.

Jonas grinned before tackling me against the comforter, his lips a searing heat against mine. I arched into him, pressing my aching nipples against his chest in a plea for some friction.

"Eager, are we?" Jonas asked, dipping his fingers inside me. "Fuck, Briar, you're absolutely dripping for me." He withdrew his fingers before bringing them up to my mouth and I opened obligingly, sucking hungrily against his slippery skin. The taste had my eyes rolling back as I moaned around him.

I felt his cock straining against my thigh, the hard length rutting softly against the tender flesh. I gripped him, impatient to have him inside me at last. We had traveled a long way, and I *ached* for him.

We both sighed as he entered me, slowly pushing inside until our hips met in a kiss. We stayed like that for a moment, just taking in the utter stillness of the room. My fingers trailed across Jonas' full lips and skittered over his cheeks as his eyes fluttered shut.

"I love you," I whispered.

The past six months had been a joyous whirlwind, our coven finally enjoying the peace that had been promised so long ago. I could hardly contain the elation I felt every time a thrum flew down the bond that connected us, hardly believing this was my life.

"I love you too, my star." Jonas' lips brushed against mine as he began pumping into me, slow and soft. When it was just Jonas and I, this was what I craved, the intimacy of our bodies moving in synchronicity together, slow and sure. He tended to my flesh like it was an altar to worship at, the ever-loving supplicants placing offerings at the base of their goddess.

Jonas sat up, bringing my knees to my chest and hitting that spot deep inside that had stars blooming in my vision. His hands wrapped around my knees as his pace picked up, stroking inside me with a guttural groan.

I knew neither of us would last very long, but we did have all afternoon, so I didn't mind as much when the spiraling heat overtook my body, and I shuddered around him with a soft release.

"Good girl," Jonas ground out, "You come so prettily around my cock. You're absolutely dripping for me, Briar, gods above."

I grinned up at him, folding my legs until they wrapped around his hips, and pulled him closer to me for a kiss. My arms tangled around his shoulders as I threaded my fingers through his curls to bring him in deeper.

Jonas' hips bucked into me as he lost control, gasping into my mouth as his hands kneaded my breasts. His fingers plucked and pulled at my tender flesh until we soared together, our shared release spilling out between our thighs as Jonas murmured sweet nothings into my hair.

His breaths came in short gasps as he sat up, drawing himself from me with a gush of wet, sticky release. I stared down at his half-hard cock and the wetness gathered at his tip. Sitting up until Jonas fell back, I took him into my mouth, licking and cleaning him until he began moaning and thrusting up into me again.

"Ah, fuck, Briar, gods you feel so good. Oh, you're so good, ah!" Jonas cried out.

He lost that last thread of control then, and his bucking became erratic as he pounded into me over and over again. I held onto his hips, holding still for him to plunder my mouth. I moaned as his cock hit the back of my throat, the vibrations adding to the sensations around him. I snaked my hand between my thighs and rubbed at myself, moaning around his cock.

Jonas' soft cry was the only precursor to the release that now slid down my throat, but I beamed up at him, all sweaty and tear streaked as he came down from another orgasm. Pure adoration shined down at me as I licked my lips clean, not wanting to waste a single drop.

"You are absolutely perfect," Jonas murmured.

We snuggled together, content to trade stories and giggles about our lives until we fell into each other again.

An afternoon well spent.

The conservatory was lush in the high peak of summer, and no matter how much the hired air elementals wafted currents through it, it didn't help quell the scorching summer heat. I was glad for the thin dress I wore, even though my skin began to mist with perspiration. I shivered as I remembered Jonas licking a long stripe between my breasts, catching the drops of condensation our love-making had created there.

"Quit it. We're about to have lunch with my mother," Jonas whispered, although a ghost of a smile drifted across his lips and a faint tug down the bond told me he was thinking about our time together just as much as I was.

"If Ian's stories have any merit, your mother would barely bat an eyelash if she knew what we'd been up to," I teased. Jonas' flush deepened, more from embarrassment than the heat, and it sent a thrill up my spine at the sight.

Ameia's warm laugh echoed through the greenery, but there were deeper, murmuring voices. Familiar voices…

Cal's face split into a fierce grin as he prowled towards me, sweeping me out of Jonas' arms and into his. "Surprise, darling," he said into my hair, settling us back to earth.

"What–" I started, glancing around to the rest of my coven. Evin's stoic face was graced with a rare, full smile, one he only sent my way, and flutters erupted in my chest at the sight. Avan and Ian were there too, deep in conversation with Ameia until Jonas and I walked up.

Ian elbowed Cal out of the way, taking both Jonas and me into his arms in a tight embrace. "Hello, little bird," he said in that sultry way of his. I would have melted on the spot, if it weren't for Ameia clearing her throat.

"It seems that my plan worked after all, hmm, Avan?" She nudged his side, startling him from where his gaze was trained on me. He cleared his throat, nodding before he made his way through the coven to stop in front of me to take my hands in his.

"Hello, sweet girl," he whispered.

"Hi," I said back, still processing what in the world was happening.

Avan cleared his throat, tossing a terrified glance at Cal before focusing back on me. "Briar, through all these trials and tribulations we've survived with each other. Leaning on our kinship and love has been the most rewarding thing of my life. I thought I knew what I wanted as a young man: power, money, infamy. That all pales in comparison to what you and this coven bring into my life. I had been lost for so long before your light shined against my face like a beam of hope. Your powers are nothing compared to the light you bring into our lives. So, I have one question–" A throat clearing from Cal interrupted his speech. "Um, *we* all have a question we would like to ask you."

The nervous energy was cloying as Avan pulled himself together.

Ameia was practically bouncing on her feet as her eyes moved from where Avan and I stood and bounced between her son, Ian, and myself. Her joy was infectious, and slowly, I could feel Avan embracing her waves of energy.

"Briar, would you join us as one, in front of magic and the kingdom itself?" Avan asked.

I felt my heart leap into my chest at his words. Yes, we'd *unofficially* been a coven for quite some time now but hearing the words made me want to soar into the sky. My magic crackled around us as my control slipped for just a moment, but in that moment, sparks flew. Flowers bloomed from the plants surrounding us, and the air was almost sweeter as a soft whisper of wind tore through the conservatory.

"Yes! Of course, yes!" I nodded vigorously, tears springing into my eyes. My coven surrounded me as our bond thrummed to life, golden sparks flying from wherever our skin connected. Finally, mine.

The wayward knight.

The stolen prince.

The broody captain.

The fiery soldier.

The promised king.

All mine, until the end of time.

ALSO BY ZOE ABRAMS

Standalones

Variance

Witches of Alehem Duology

The Crescent Spell

The Moonlit Dance

Paranormal Monster Romance with Lana Kole

The Abdominal Snowman

ACKNOWLEDGEMENTS

Wow! Briar's story is finally done. This was a labor of love, and I hope that you loved her story as much as I enjoyed writing it.

I wouldn't have been able to do this without the support of my loving husband, J. His faith in me to finish this story was really the push that I needed to punch out these words. I love you honey! Your support means everything.

To my bestie extraordinaire! Your cheering from the sidelines and helpful comments are what took MD from here to HERE, and I'm so thankful that the bookverse brought us together. I can't wait to squeeze the ever loving shit out of you!

Alexa – You came in at the midnight hour and worked so hard on the edits for MD, and I cannot thank you enough. Your keen eye was the cherry on top, and I don't think MD would be what it is without you. You'll never get rid of me now.

Rachel – gosh I love TikTok. I found your gorgeous art there and it led me to the two most beautiful covers I could've asked for. I'm so thankful for your kind words and for running with my idea of "I dunno, I trust you!" You're never getting rid of me either.

And finally, to you, my beautiful readers. I'm so incredibly thankful for all of the support through my ups and downs (and when I disappear off the face of the planet for weeks at a time). Your cheers through this writing process have fueled me to create something that I can be proud of, and I hope you are too. Thank you, from the bottom of my heart.

ABOUT ZOE ABRAMS

Zoe Abrams resides in the sometimes warm, but mostly cold, central region of Michigan. She is happily married to a human man and has produced two offspring, which she is immensely proud of. Zoe writes all kinds of romance books, but they mostly tend to be on the sweeter side and *always* spicy. She enjoys reading, of course, journaling, knitting, cooking, and all things witchy. You'll most likely find her curled up with her heated blanket, a cup of tea, and a good book in the best lighting in her house. For aesthetic purposes.

FOLLOW ZOE ON SOCIAL MEDIA!

Facebook Group @ The Abrams Collective

Instagram and TikTok @ authorzoeabrams

Printed in Great Britain
by Amazon